The Weed Eater

by

Edward S. Baker

*Bartholomew Jones Series, Book
Three*

Cover Art by *Tina Lynn Stout*

The Wild Rose Press, Inc.
PO Box 708
Adams Basin, NY 14410-0708
Visit us at www.thewildrosepress.com

Publishing History
First Edition, 2024
Trade Paperback ISBN 978-1-5092-5611-2
Digital ISBN 978-1-5092-5612-9

Bartholomew Jones Series, Book Three
Published in the United States of America

Dedication

This novel is dedicated to those who work tirelessly to keep invasive weeds from encroaching upon small recreational lakes.

Acknowledgements

Many thanks to my wife, Edna, for helping keep my writing on the straight and narrow. And thanks, as well, to my editor, Ally Robertson, whose expert eye catches the glitches and typos that have escaped my own.

Chapter One

El Serpiente reflected on the procedures he had conducted on the two captives. He had driven splinters under their fingernails. He had poured acid onto their testicles. He had drilled into their teeth until his bit found the nerve, and then he had applied ice water. Next, he had stabbed their eyeballs with hot needles and driven screws into their kneecaps. Both men had screamed in pain time and again, but neither had given up the information El Serpiente wanted. Perhaps they did not know what he sought. In the end, it was too late. The Angel of Mercy descended from the sky and took the souls of the men to a hacienda in another world where they would find comfort in the arms of their savior.

"What you want done with the bodies?" Ramon asked.

"Burn them or grind them," El Serpiente replied. "It doesn't matter. If that cannot be done, hide them where nobody will find them."

"Si," Ramon replied. He made the sign of the cross over the dead men and then helped Pasquale wrap them in a tarp.

When the bodies had been securely packaged, the two men loaded them into the bed of a rusty El Camino and threw bags of manure on top of them. Ramon started the motor with a rumble. The truck needed a new muffler.

As the tires of the El Camino spit stones against its rubber mud flaps outside his home, El Serpiente turned on the Hallmark Channel and snuggled beside his five-year-old daughter. "This one is *Love in Iceland*. Someday I'll take you there. Their horses are something special."

****

Ramon and Pasquale worked through the chill of the New York morning in Pasquale's back yard on a country road near Voorheesville High School. Pasquale had felled an oak tree a week before and had rented a light-duty woodchipper to turn its small branches into mulch for his flower gardens. The chipper was also a perfect way to mulch the bodies of two dead hombres. Except for the knee bones.

Pasquale used his machete to cut the first body into bite-sized chunks to feed into the chipper. Ramon dropped each piece in, alternating meat and bone with branches from the oak tree. He watched in awe as the shredder sent chips of brown wood into a pile, and then in wonder as tiny bits of red and white filled the air with pink dust which settled upon the chips of brown. When all that remained were the knees and the skull, Ramon dropped the first knee bone into the shredder's mouth. The shredder moaned and bucked as its blades tried in vain to shatter the bone. Then it smoked for a moment and died. Just like that.

"Now what we going to do, amigo?" Pasquale asked.

Ramon tried to pry the knee bone from the grip of the shredder's blades. It was no use. "We gonna pour gasoline onto this machine and burn it until it is unrecognizable. Then we gonna to go ask for our money back."

"No, Ramon. I mean what we going to do with that head and this other body?"

****

By five o'clock, night had begun to fall. Pasquale and Ramon loaded the second body and the head of the first into the bed of the El Camino. As they drove west, a dark line of clouds filled the sky and snow began to fall. Heavy snow.

The two men found a deserted stretch of secondary road high above the village of Mariaville. Pasquale pulled onto the right shoulder and shut the El Camino's motor. They removed the second body from the tarp and plopped it onto the snow at their feet. Pasquale severed its head with three swings of his machete. Then they lifted the body and tossed it over the guardrail and onto a steep embankment. It rolled away into the darkness. Ramon took the severed head and tossed it into the drainage ditch on the other side of the road.

Headlights appeared in the distance. An unknown vehicle was climbing the road behind them. The men quickly climbed back into their El Camino and continued along the road until they came to a small bridge which crossed a creek.

"Stop here, Ramon," Pasquale cried.

Ramon pressed on his brakes and the El Camino drifted to a slow stop in the deepening snow.

Pasquale stepped out and removed a paper bag from the El Camino's bed. He tossed the bag and the head it contained into the creek below. Then he climbed back into the warmth of the El Camino's cab. "Time to go home, Ramon."

Ramon turned the El Camino in a tight arc and

headed back in the direction they had come. Half a mile down the road a county snowplow passed them going in the opposite direction. A continuous wedge of snow flew from the plow's blade and onto the roadside.

"Think that plow hid the body, Ramon?"

"Si, Pasquale. Nobody's going to find the body out here. You see any houses?"

"No. This is a good place to deposit things we don't need."

Chapter Two

My name is Bartholomew Jones, detective on unexpected furlough from the Willow Falls Police Department. I was driving back to my cabin on Mariaville Lake when my cell phone rang. It was Caesar French, the new CEO of Cabrillo Construction, Inc., a local corporation that had appeared in Willow Falls and quickly risen into prominence over the past three years.

"Is that you, Jones? I heard you got a couple days off."

Obviously, like his predecessor, French had an inside informant at the police department. "Yeah. It's a miscarriage of justice. You calling to rub it in?"

"Nope. I know you did a couple of jobs for Diego Cisneros when he was head of Cabrillo. I got job for you to do…if you're interested."

I looked in my rearview mirror, saw nobody was behind me, and pulled my tan sedan to the right shoulder of the road. After an eighteen-wheeler blew by me on its way to Schenectady, I rechecked my side view mirror and then did a U-turn toward French's office and the possibility of a payday.

I slammed my palm on my steering wheel. Only a few days ago, Chief Comstock had placed me on a week's rip because he had learned I was moonlighting as a private investigator. A rip is a paid disciplinary furlough with reduced pay. If I had not agreed to the furlough, I would have had to take my chances in court, where I could get fewer days or a harsher penalty. Cops almost always lose in court, so I agreed to the furlough. The real kicker is for every day I am on furlough, I lose a day of vacation. That really sucks.

After thanking me for helping solve a murder committed by a local blood drinking cult, Chief Comstock had read me the riot act. "Article Fifteen of the Department's collective bargaining agreement with the City of Willow Falls prohibits all police officers from taking a part-time job without prior approval."

"Screw the damn union contract," I replied. "It's nobody's business what I do when I'm not on duty as a detective."

He held out his hand. "Give me your piece and your badge. I'll see you in a week. Bring your union representative with you when you come back. And be sure to make an appointment."

I handed him my badge and laid my Sig service weapon on his desktop. "This really sucks, Chief."

He pointed at the door.

I slammed it when I left his office.

How was I going to survive without my part-time job? Hell, my wife Rachel was suing me for divorce, demanding both our home and alimony. I needed the extra money my part-time job provided because after I paid the mortgage and power bills and bought Rachel groceries, I couldn't live on the remaining two hundred dollars per month.

Chief Comstock was being totally unfair. I had taken on only one investigative job. It was for French's predecessor, Diego Cisneros, who had lost a commodity and needed help discovering which one of three employees had taken it. When I identified the culprit and explained the type of business he had opened, Cisneros thanked me because it provided Cabrillo Construction an entirely new avenue to make money from the entrepreneurial ingenuity of one of its employees. Who would have thought Albany, New York, would be home to a hotbed of interest in cockfighting?

I arrived at Cabrillo Construction and was greeted warmly by the receptionist, a buxom young woman with blonde hair and dark black roots. Her name was Laverne.

"He's over in Building Three. You can wait for him here or go on over there by yourself. I gotta watch the phones."

"Thank you."

I headed across the tarmac to Building Three. The wind was blowing flurries from the west at twenty miles per hour, and the chill factor had to be in the teens. I zipped my woolen jacket up to my neck, put my hands in its pockets, and pushed into the wind.

Like all the buildings which surrounded it, Building Three was a warehouse sided in dusty brown steel with a green roof which gently sloped at a ten-degree angle. Both ends housed garage doors large enough to accompany an eighteen-wheeler, and its sides offered a couple of doors for those who arrive on foot. I entered a side door.

Inside, I saw French talking with a man who was holding a paint gun in his hand. Beside them stood a large garbage truck, the kind that has a claw on its side to lift containers until their contents are emptied into a gaping hole on top of its cylindrical body. The cab of the truck had been painted black, and its driver's side door had been airbrushed with the word "Scentless" in silver.

The remainder of the truck had been sandblasted to its bare steel, obviously waiting for the painter to finish his work.

The painter pointed in my direction. French looked up and waved. He returned his attention to the painter for another few seconds and then walked to me, holding out his hand. "Is that you, Jones?"

I nodded.

"Glad to meet you. You want some coffee? The beans just arrived from Jamaica—French roast."

"Sure. Black, please."

He escorted me into a small office in the back of the warehouse. The six small panes in the hollow-bodied office door had been painted black. Screwed across them was a piece of plywood which had been spray-painted black with the words "Scentless Waste Removal" hand lettered in silver.

I sat down in the steel folding chair on the guest side of the office's desk. "I gather you're now in the waste removal business."

French removed his royal blue quilted vest, then poured two cups of coffee and handed me one in a white ceramic mug. "Yes, it's a new business venture which promises to be very lucrative. Everybody's got trash and somebody's got to haul it away. Why not Scentless?"

"Is this why you asked me to come in today?"

"Unfortunately, I have a bigger problem than trash, I think. You're a private detective, and I could use your expertise."

I nodded and waited.

French sipped his coffee. "There's nothing like fresh-roasted Jamaican beans."

I sipped mine. "Yeah. This is different from the stuff

you get in the grocery store."

He smiled briefly and then his expression became serious. "So, here's my problem…"

I took a small notebook and pen from inside my coat and looked up.

"I got two guys…employees…missing. Their disappearance makes me worry about a war."

His comment piqued my interest. "What makes you say that?"

"There are too many of us trying to make a living here."

I scratched my head with the end of my pen. "Too many people?"

French nodded. "Yes, too many men and too many businesses claiming the same territory. It has happened before, especially in New Jersey, where there was enough money to be made by all, but some got greedy and wanted more than their fair share. Violence began and it brought the FBI into the state."

My knowledge of troubles in New Jersey was as deep as a layer of cellophane. "The FBI was called in?"

"Yes. There were several murders involving the New Jersey mob, as recently as 2015, but also back in 1995 and even in 1983."

"It sounds awful, especially since businessmen were involved."

French nodded. "It was."

I shook my head. "I'm sorry I don't pay much attention to news from other states."

I needed more details about his missing employees. "What can you tell me about the two missing men? Do you suspect they've been kidnapped or killed? Is it possible they've gone into hiding somewhere, perhaps afraid of you or somebody else?"

"My men have nothing to fear from me, as long as they do their work and are honest."

He handed me two sheets of paper with photos and background information about both men. I gave them a quick once-over. They looked like mugshots because neither guy was smiling. Chico Herrera was from Morelia, Mexico, wherever that was. His primary job function was trash truck driver. Jorge Perez was from Campeche, another city in Mexico which meant nothing to me. He had recently begun work as ombudsman to the cockfighting arena in Albany. I took "ombudsman" to mean he collected trash and dead roosters for disposal…and maybe cash. I suspected the arena might be a good place to start my investigation.

"Is there anything else you can think of to help me…maybe distinguishing physical characteristics?"

"Jorge wears a gold cap on his left front tooth. It has a diamond mounted right in its center. When he smiles, you can't miss it."

"And how long have they been missing?"

"Since Saturday. Jorge never showed up after Friday night's cockfights. Chico shares an apartment with Jorge in 'Little Havana' and may have gone to the cockfights with him, but I haven't been able to verify that." He looked at me inquisitively. "I haven't given you very much to go on, have I?"

I tilted my head in agreement. "Both of these men are Mexicans. Are they illegals?"

"Contrary to appearances, my employees are all new Americans. Most are refugees from persecution by foreign despots. All are seeking asylum and eventual citizenship. I work with several national and international human service organizations to bring them to the United States. I give them minimum wages jobs, but I also provide free housing. The federal and state governments provide food stamps, medical insurance, transportation allowances, and job training. It's a win-win for everyone."

"Until something unusual happens to one of them."

"Yes. In this case, to two of them." He wiped his brow with a handkerchief. "Do you speak Spanish or Vietnamese?"

"No. I took Latin in high school, but I don't remember much of it."

"In this business, the ability to speak multiple foreign languages is a necessity. Your dependence upon English may handicap your ability to solve this case."

I nodded thoughtfully.

"I wish you God speed in finding my two employees. The immigrant community is wary of police and investigators of any kind. This case may be more difficult than you anticipate."

"It's a start, and I'll get right on it." But he was right. I don't speak Spanish and I stick out like a strawberry in a blueberry bowl when I'm in an ethnic community. Finding these men was not going to be easy. I would have to call in some assistance, probably my old friend Mescal.

Chapter Three

I waited a couple of days, and then I called Helen
Martin. She and I had worked a couple of cases recently,
and our friendship had been growing stronger. It was
mid-morning, and I could picture her behind her desk
pretending to be working on a case when she was really
looking for discount deals on nice clothes on the internet.

"Yeah?" she screeched into the phone.

"Helen, it's Bart. Did I catch you at a bad time?"

"Yeah, you did, you sorry bastard. I just flushed the
toilet in the third-floor ladies' room. It's clogged and
overflowing. Some valve must be stuck or something."

"So, call me back when you catch a break, okay?"

She hung up without saying "Goodbye."

I was washing a couple of pairs of socks in the
kitchen sink when she returned my call an hour later.
"You always pick the most inconvenient times for a
social call," she said. "What did you want, anyway?"

"I could tell you were in some sort of distress. Did
you get the pipes fixed?"

"Yeah. Sergeant Dombrowski heard us screaming—
me and the fat girl from Records—and he came into the
bathroom with his piece drawn. When he saw what was
happening, he kicked the valve seat behind the toilet.
That freed it up and the water stopped running."

"Sounds pretty bad…"

"Yeah, I guess there was some damage down on the

second floor, but none in my office. I'm grateful for that." She paused a moment. "Well, what did you want?"

"I'm trying to chase down some information on two guys. You got a pencil?"

"You doing more of your private eye stuff?"

"Yeah. It's missing persons' stuff. If I give you their names, can you see if they're anywhere in the system?"

"Sure, I s'pose. You taking a nice girl out to lunch today?"

"Sure, I s'pose," I said, mocking her African-American vernacular. "You got a hankerin' for fish?"

"That would be nice. See you there, or are you driving me?"

"Well, I…"

"Yeah, you're right. You aren't supposed to be hanging around the department, so I'll meet you there. How about twelve thirty?"

"Sounds good."

"Now, how about those names?"

"Both are Hispanic. Mexican, I think. The first one is Chico Herrera. The other one is Jorge Perez. You spell Jorge with a J, not an H."

"I know that, Jonesy. You think I'm illiterate or something?"

"Sorry, just making sure you didn't spell it wrong. They're roommates in an apartment in Little Havana. I'll text you the address in a few minutes. It's out in the car."

"I'll see if I can find them without an address, first. It'll be a good test run for the new database system."

"New system? I've been gone for less than a week and the chief already has a new system?"

"Why do you think he sent you packing? He needed enough money to tip the movers and installation guys.

Gave them maybe five dollars each."

I smiled. Helen was fooling with me, so we were still cool. "Okay, see you at twelve thirty at Captain Mambo's. Bring your appetite."

"Have I ever left it behind when somebody else is buying?"

I arrived at Captain Mambo's a few minutes before twelve thirty but decided to wait for Helen before going in. It was a place which catered to anybody with a couple of dollars, but most of its clientele were people of color who didn't like sharing their dining space with white bread types, unless they were accompanied by someone of color. It always amazed me Helen didn't mind bringing me into the place, except she once told me she only did it because I was paying. I hoped she was kidding.

Helen arrived in her Hyundai at exactly twelve thirty. She was wearing a gold-colored full-length wool coat with a leopard print fur collar and matching hat.

I stepped out of my sedan and waved. "I didn't recognize you at first. I thought you were a Vogue model."

She smiled. "Cut the crap, Jonesy. No matter how many compliments you throw my way, you're still paying the tab."

I held the door for her, and we walked into the humid inside air. It smelled fishy.

Helen blazed a trail through an array of square tables and up to the counter. I followed close behind, hoping not too many patrons would be offended by my presence in their culinary sanctuary.

The woman behind the counter was dressed in a blue shirt with a Captain Mambo logo. Her hair was netted.

Her white plastic name tag bore the same logo, but her name had been scrawled in magic marker on a strip of adhesive tape.

"I'll have Captain Mambo plate," Helen said. "And a glass of iced tea, no sugar."

"Hi, Althea," I said. "Make mine a steamed shrimp and gumbo platter. I'll have sweetened tea."

"Do I know you?"

I pointed at her name tag. "It was a giveaway."

She rolled her eyes. "You want cornbread?"

"Sure."

"How 'bout your girlfriend?"

"You should ask her yourself."

Helen pursed her lips and shot me a dirty look. "Yeah, I'll have cornbread. If you got any honey packets, I'd like two."

Althea tilted her head and looked at me.

"Sure. Would you happen to have Tupelo or Sourwood?"

"We got honey. That's all it says."

"Sure."

When Althea took our orders into the kitchen, Helen elbowed me in the gut. "Why you always causing trouble, Jonesy? You ain't been introduced to the young lady, so you don't go calling her by her first name, even if it is on a nametag."

"Black culture?"

"Common decency, you uncultured buffoon." Helen straightened her shoulders and brushed against me. "And honey is honey."

"Like beer is beer?"

"You gonna ask for a wheatberry brown ale in an establishment like this?"

She had a point.

Helen found us a small table for two away from the other patrons, several of whom were watching every move we made. The waitress brought our drinks.

"Thank you," I said.

She nodded.

"What you doing now, Jonesy?" Helen asked when the waitress departed. "Who's your client?"

"Are you asking because you're going to report back to the chief?"

"You know me better than that."

"Yeah, I do." I took a sip of iced tea. "It's like this, Helen: My client asked me to sign a non-disclosure agreement, so I have to honor it. I'd love to tell you about him and my investigation, but legally I can't."

"But you don't mind calling me to get information which only can come from police databases?"

"Yeah, something like that."

The waitress brought us our meals. My bowl of gumbo was steaming hot, and my shrimp were still warm and ready to be dipped in Captain Mambo's famous lime-based sauce. Helen's platter had a little of everything—shrimp, fish, crawdads, slaw, and hushpuppies. It looked delicious, and I wondered if I should have ordered it instead of what I did. However, I love gumbo and Helen's plate didn't include any.

Helen took a bite of fried fish and then began lecturing me again. "Don't you see how being a private eye is a conflict of interest with your police work? In fact, you don't have the skills to be a private eye without access to police information systems."

"You know I have financial obligations due to my pending divorce. On a normal basis, I need the part-time job so I won't starve. But when Chief Comstock put me on unpaid leave, he left me no choice but to continue and maybe expand my private investigation work or else I can't meet my obligations."

She pointed a finger at me. "They coming after you, Jonesy. You're a maverick. You don't play by anybody's rules…not the city's and not the union's."

I looked in her eyes and shrugged. But I knew she was right about me.

"I used to have a thing for you, but I don't have time for some guy who's planning on collecting coins in a can on a street corner when this is all over. I didn't know you play the guitar. You sing, too? There's a nice corner down by the bus station. Got your name on it if you want it."

"Can it, would you. You're going to give me indigestion."

I peeled another shrimp and stuffed it into my mouth. I hoped Helen wasn't correct about my future, and I didn't like hearing "they" were coming after me. In reality, I needed both jobs. Being a city detective gave me a steady income, health insurance, and a retirement plan. Being a private detective gave me extra spending money, but that was about it. I wished I could win the New York lottery, but I didn't have enough spare change to waste on lottery tickets.

Helen changed the subject. "I did a little research on those fellas you asked about."

"Already?"

"Well, I had some time this morning and the new database was waiting for someone to ask it some questions. I figured it might as well be me."

"What did you learn?"

"No surprises. They're both illegals, but both have qualified with the state for driver's licenses. They both get food stamps and free medical, thanks to New York State government policies. I figure they're lying about their incomes."

"What makes you say that?"

"Both have savings accounts in excess of thirty-thousand dollars at Willow Falls National Bank."

"Wow. It pays to be an illegal, doesn't it?"

"I guess so, especially since their income tax returns don't list any form of employment."

"Really?"

"Scout's honor."

I knew Herrera and Perez both work for French, so he must be paying them in cash under the table. It is common knowledge that every check a bank touches today is scanned. So, if French paid by check, there would be a trail of cancelled checks at the bank. I was certain there wouldn't be.

Chapter Four

I drove to 1362 Van Rensselaer Drive and pulled
into one of three empty parking spaces in front of the old
vacuum cleaner repair shop, now the headquarters of the
Willow Falls chapter of the Mexican Banditos. Its leader,
Pedro "Mescal" Herrera, and I had become
acquaintances of sorts. He had given me just enough
information to help me solve a couple of cases which did
not incriminate him or his gang, and I got him released
from jail when he was arrested on illegal weapons
charges. I guess it was a symbiotic relationship of sorts.
We were almost friends.

I got out of my sedan and walked carefully across
the jagged ice on the sidewalk. As I did, I saw the front
curtain open and quickly close. From inside I heard
someone say, "Hey, Mescal, it's that cop."

The building's plywood front door still was painted
with a black Death's head. As I reached out to knock on
it, it opened. It was Mescal. "Hey, gringo. Long time no
see. Whatcha doin' for work nowadays?"

"Obviously you know I'm on unpaid leave?"

"Si, hombre. Wha' you do to have them treat you
like that?"

I zipped up my coat. "Can I come in? It's damn cold
out today."

Mescal shook his head. "You know you can't come
inside. You gotta be a member. How 'bout we talk in

your ride?"

I nodded and walked carefully to get back into my car. As I did, I complained to him. "You gotta do better cleaning the ice off your sidewalks, Mescal. That stuff is treacherous."

"I keep my sidewalks this way 'cause I don' want nobody trying to peek into my windows. It's like building a lake around my castle, 'cept the water is frozen and tromped on to make it uneven."

Mescal opened the passenger's side door and climbed in. "This is some piece of shit car, gringo. Aren't you working for French now? You should be driving a Jag."

"I'm still a cop, Mescal. I'm just on a leave of absence."

Mescal smiled and nodded. Maybe he knew more about my future than I did. "Wha' you want today? I am always at your service."

"How's my buddy Diablo?" Diablo was a rooster Mescal had raised for competition in the cockfighting ring in Albany.

"He's in retirement now. He won eleven straight matches and then got the shit kicked out of him by a big brown son of a bitch some Puerto Rican imported. It wasn't no fair fight. Diablo lost an eye, but he can still score with the ladies. I got three of his offspring in training right now. One of them is gonna kill that brown bastard."

"Too bad about his eye. The hens must think he's winking at them."

"You know, I never thought of that. No wonder he gets so much time in the sack."

Mescal's breath was fogging up my windshield, so

I turned on my motor. He looked panicked for a moment.

"Relax," I said. "I'm just warming up the interior and defogging my windshield."

The tension in Mescal's neck and hands eased a little.

"I need your help, Mescal. I'm looking for a couple of men who work for French. They've disappeared. Thought maybe you'd know something about it."

"Why didn't he come to me hisself? We got a special arrangement ever since some of his new guys joined the Banditos. You know about that?"

"No, I don't know anything about that. Maybe he wants to keep it low key. Maybe he doesn't want you thinking he cares about his peons."

Mescal turned toward me, his left knee resting on the console between our two seats. "French is a good boss, gringo. He's like me. His eyes water whenever one of his men is hurt."

"Do you know Jorge Perez or Chico Herrera?"

"Jorge? Is he the hombre French stationed at the cockfighting arena when the prices went up?"

"Yes, that would be him."

"He was a bastardo. He thought he owned the place. Thought he was the boss and not Prognostico. Maybe Julio put a hit on him."

Before French took over Cabrillo Construction, it was managed by Diego Cisneros. Julio Prognostico was Diego Cisneros' godson, so I didn't think he would have had Perez killed. But Prognostico was not above criminal acts. After all, he was the guy who stole some of Cisneros' merchandise and sold it to purchase and convert an empty warehouse into the capital region's only cockfighting arena—all behind his godfather's back. When Cisneros learned what Prognostico had done, he demanded a piece of the action as well as financial retribution. Now that French was in charge of Cabrillo Construction, it always was possible Prognostico could have had Perez eliminated out of anger at having to continue to pay tribute to Cabrillo.

"Are you still friends with Prognostico?" I asked.

"Si, gringo."

"Do you think you could get me in to chat with him?"

"As a private investigator for the guy who replaced his godfather? I don't think so. Might get you killed."

"But he may hold the key to Perez's disappearance. He may know where Perez is hiding."

"*If* Perez is hiding and not muerto." Mescal held his hands to his face as if he were praying. "I may have something better. Wait here. I'll be right back."

Mescal got out of my car and went back inside his headquarters. Three minutes later he came back out, accompanied by another guy. Mescal opened the back door and motioned for the guy to get in. Mescal sat beside him.

"Gringo, this is my friend Henrico. Tha's not his real name, but you can call him that. Until recently, he was a trash truck driver."

I nodded. "Ola, Henrico."

Henrico nodded at me. He was tall and young. His black denim jeans and sleeveless jacket fit him as though they were two sizes too small, especially in leg and sleeve length. His pointed goatee was thin and short.

"Henrico, this hombre is my friend, Mr. Jones. You can call him 'Mr. Jones.' You got to tell him what you tol' me about the trash business."

Henrico nodded again but did not say anything to me.

"Go on," Mescal prompted. "Tell him everything."

Henrico thought for a moment and then began. "I worked for Onondaga Trash Company until last Friday. It's the largest trash company in this region."

"Yes, I know that."

"There is a war coming, Mr. Jones."

French had told me the same thing a couple of days ago. "I've heard that from someone else, too."

"Onondaga Trash has employed Los Cuernos to help eliminate its competition through intimidation."

"Los Cuernos? Really?" I asked.

Henrico squirmed in his seat. "Si. It means 'The Horns'…Satan's horns."

The Los Cuernos gang had been a problem on Long Island for more than ten years, often launching killing sprees, but I was not aware they had migrated. "I didn't know they were up here."

"They are. They were hired to intimidate others, except they been killing drivers and crews of trucks operated by the other trash companies."

"Really? Have the other companies reported these murders to the police?"

"This place is going to be another Sinaloa. Nobody trusts the police. The businesses will settle this by themselves."

I knew Sinaloa is a state in Mexico where drug cartels went to war against the Mexican government. The Mexican Marines captured one of the cartel's leaders but had to release him when all the warring cartels banded together to fight the Marines in a war that killed many civilians. I looked at Mescal. He nodded in agreement.

"Have you heard of Scentless Waste Removal?" I asked.

"Si. That company is headed by 'El Escondido.'"

I wasn't familiar with the name. "Not French?"

"French *is* 'El Escondido,' gringo," Mescal said. "It means 'The Hidden One.' "

Henrico continued. "El Escondido has been growing his business and getting new trucks by ambushing trash truck drivers from other companies across New York, New Jersey, and Ohio."

"Really?"

"Si. His men, they pull drivers out of their trucks under threat of death. They take the drivers' cell phones and then leave the drivers in deserted places along the highway. Then his men use back roads to move the stolen trucks to his warehouse here in town, where he cleans them up and repaints them shiny black."

Mescal looked at me. "French is not doing anything bad. The companies he steals from have stolen their trucks from others. Tha's the way it's done. And he's growing a legal business. Have you seen the ads on television? He's offering free trash removal for six months for new customers."

No wonder French seemed happy about his new enterprise when we spoke the other day. Without the cost of purchasing new trucks, he had amassed a new fleet and created a new business for almost nothing. And business seemed to be booming. But his methods might be spurring a war. And I just learned that French had a nickname: El Escondido. Was he possibly connected to a cartel the way Cisneros was? If so, I possibly was in deeper shit than I had imagined.

Chapter Five

It was the end of my rip, and I was due to meet with Chief Comstock for reinstatement. I found my copy of the union contract and looked up the name of my representative, George Hughes. I called him "Fat Georgie," and he knew it. I couldn't see him being much help, but I called him anyway.

He must have had caller ID on his phone. "Oh, it's you, Jones," he said before even greeting me with a "Hello."

"Yeah, Georgie. My rip is ending, and I need you to accompany me to a meeting with Comstock." A rip is a forced vacation from work—with pay, if you're fortunate enough to have accrued a pile of vacation days. I wasn't so fortunate.

"When?"

"I haven't set it up yet, but Monday would probably be the best date."

"Make it for Tuesday"

The S.O.B. was busting my balls. That would mean a sixth day of rip and the loss of another vacation day.

"Why's that?"

"Comstock's off on Monday. He's getting some kind of award at a luncheon in Albany at noon Monday."

"Well, then, I'll be back at work on Monday. I'm not losing any more vacation days. Five is enough."

"I wouldn't do that if I were you. The contract is

pretty clear you can't come back to work until Comstock approves it. If he's not there, there's no approval. Capice?"

"Yeah. You're both busting my balls. I'll call you with the day and time of the meeting." I hung up.

I called Comstock's secretary. "Hey, Louise. It's Bart Jones."

"Oh hello, Detective Jones. The Chief told me to expect your call. He's suggesting a meeting at one p.m. on Tuesday."

"I guess it'll have to do. Put me down for one p.m. George Hughes will be joining us."

"Yes, I already spoke to him yesterday and he said he'd be there."

So, Fat Georgie already knew the day and time of our meeting with the chief, and he could have given me the information himself. I couldn't stand the guy, and this was another reason why.

****

Tuesday morning arrived. The wind was howling out of the west, blowing loose snow from the lake against the sliding glass doors of my cabin. I knew I would be walking around the cabin in a few days and shoveling the drifts away from the doors if I ever hoped to open them before Spring. Valentine's Day was a week away, but I figured Cupid would not be able to fly against these winds, so I would skip sending anyone a card, especially my estranged wife Rachel.

The mailman stopped at my rural route box at ten, and I trudged out to see if he had brought me any good news. As luck would have it, he had not. The small handful of mail included circulars from two grocery stores and a nine by twelve manilla envelope from Lester

Brockbank, my attorney.

Back inside my cabin, I poured my third cup of coffee for the day and opened the manilla envelope. It was my copy of the official divorce decree from the State of New York, including a breakdown of my responsibilities for Rachel's well-being. I was to pay the mortgage on the home where she currently resided until such time as she should sell it, and I was to pay her a stipulated monthly support allotment until such time as she remarried or passed away.

Great. This could be a life sentence.

There was more. Upon my retirement from the police department, I was to provide her fifty percent of the amount credited for my first ten years of employment. My attorney, Les Brockbank, was going to have to help me figure out how to calculate that amount. What if I never reached retirement age? The document didn't address that possibility. At least I was not required to name her as beneficiary of my life insurance policy.

I tabulated how much of my paycheck Rachel was going to take and how much would remain for my spending pleasure. It was a simple addition and subtraction process which resulted in my seeing more of my pay than I originally had thought. Instead of trying to live on two hundred dollars per month, I was now blessed with two hundred twelve dollars. It was clear to me I needed my contract with French more than ever.

At twelve thirty I put on my dress uniform and drove into Willow Falls. When I entered the department, Georgie Hughes was waiting for me outside Chief Comstock's office. We did not shake hands.

"Hi, Georgie. Thanks for showing up."

"I'm obligated to show up. It's my job." He looked

nervous. His forehead glowed with perspiration and his neck was dappled with red splotches.

When we were called into the chief's office, I walked in first. Comstock was not alone. The city attorney and the head of Personnel were sitting at a table which had been set up in front of the chief's desk. There were two empty chairs, I presumed waiting for Georgie Hughes and me. From everyone's expression, I could tell this was not going to go well for me.

Chief Comstock motioned for us to sit down. I took the seat at the very end of the table, where I could see everyone's face and they could see mine.

"Good afternoon, everyone," the chief began. "We're here today to discuss Detective Jones' behaviors in defiance of his department's collective bargaining agreement with the city. Specifically, he has been working a part-time job without first obtaining permission to do so through official channels. It's a violation of Article Fifteen." He looked at me. "Detective Jones, do you have anything to say in your own defense?"

"This is old business, as far as I'm concerned, Chief. Yes, I took on a single client for a brief matter requiring private investigation. It did not interfere with my official duties with the city. I worked only nights and weekends for a very brief period. I took on the work because my wife and I separated. After paying her rent, groceries, and other bills, I don't have enough money left to live on."

The head of personnel cleared her throat and asked me a question without looking at me. "Who is your client, Detective Jones?"

I leaned back in my chair. If I said anything about

working for French or his predecessor, Diego Cisneros, I would be violating my contract and would probably lose my job with the city. "I'm sorry, but I signed a non-disclosure agreement which prohibits me from divulging that information."

"How are we to judge whether or not your part-time work has violated ethical standards or abridged confidentiality?"

"I would be abridging confidentiality if I gave you my client's name."

She straightened her white blouse and pulled back her chin as though I had said something offensive.

"Have you only made one single contract for private investigative work?" the chief asked.

"For the period we're discussing I made only one contract. That contract has been closed. However, I know you're going to ask me if I've taken on any additional work, and the answer is 'Yes.' Since I've been on rip and not able to conduct my duties as a police detective, I've taken on one other contract in order to meet the obligations of my divorce. The department certainly doesn't want to see one of its detectives in the newspaper for failure to comply with a court order."

"Who is your new client?" the stuffy lady from Personnel asked.

"Same problem, ma'am," I replied.

"Non-disclosure?"

"Yes."

Now it was Fat Georgie's turn. "So, you defied the intent of the rip?"

"Intent?"

"Yes, the purpose of the rip was to give you time to think about your obligation as a member of our union.

Your friends and work associates are all members of the union, and when one of us egregiously violates the contract, it reflects poorly on the rest. If you are permitted to get away with violating Article Fifteen, then everyone else in the union will believe they should be afforded the same opportunity."

I threw my hands up in the air. "It's really none of the union's business what I do when I'm off duty, as long as I am not violating the law."

Georgie slammed his hand down on the table. "The contract *is* the law, Detective Jones. Any form of investigative work is a conflict of interest and is in violation of the union contract. You've set a very bad example for all policemen."

"Give me a break, Georgie. The union is a way for everybody to be treated the same. The slackers get the same pay raises and benefits as the hard workers. I mean, look at you. How many collars did you make last year? Two? Three? Its guys like me who do the grunt work…who risk our lives to keep this city free from what people would turn it into if we weren't keeping the slime from overrunning the streets—"

"Enough, Jones," Comstock said. "We've heard quite enough. I believe your union, the department, and the city are in agreement as to the outcome of today's meeting. We'll be taking your case to the court system."

All the heads around the table nodded, except mine. I had heard about kangaroo courts before, but I had never seen one in action. Comstock and the others knew what they were going to do, and the outcome was predetermined before I had scheduled the meeting.

"Meanwhile, you're to remain on your rip until you hear from me. And *only* me."

"That could be weeks, Chief. I only have seven vacation days left."

The prune from Personnel chimed in, this time looking directly at me. "In that case, Detective Jones, when your vacation days are entirely consumed, your pay will be docked one day's pay for each day you're on the rip."

"In other words, I won't receive a paycheck after seven more days on the rip? I'll be penniless."

She smiled at me. "You should have thought about that before you started this awful business. I'm sure Sergeant Hughes would have been glad to share his thoughts with you if you had discussed your situation with him before you launched your own business on the side."

I looked at Comstock. He just shrugged his shoulders.

I jumped from my seat. "This is bullshit. I'll see you all in court." I stormed out of the room and slammed the door behind me.

Chief Comstock looked at the small committee still seated at the table. "You know, he's one of my best detectives. He solved the case of BabyX and discovered the cult of bloodsuckers. I'm going to miss him."

Chapter Six

Helen called me that evening. I didn't answer her call but decided to let it go to voicemail. I was still fuming from the meeting with Comstock, especially from the lack of support I received from my union representative, Fat Georgie Hughes. I promised myself someday I would sucker-punch that S.O.B. when he least expected it.

"Hey. Jonesy," Helen said in her voicemail. *"I heard what happened to you today. George Hughes made sure everyone in the department knows, so nobody does the same thing...you know, part-time work without prior approval...You there?...Well, call me if you'd like to talk."*

I didn't know enough swear words to express how I felt at that moment. It was better not to talk with anyone.

****

I woke up at eleven in the morning on Wednesday, but I had not fallen to sleep until after three. It had taken three bottles of beer and three or four shots of Gentleman Jack to knock me out. My sleep had been fretful, no doubt as the result of the meeting with the chief.

I took a shower to try to clear my head. Then I ate eggs and toast for lunch. And I drank three cups of coffee.

At noon, I checked my cell phone. There were two messages from Helen and one from Caesar French.

Helen's messages were in the same vein as her first: She wanted to talk whenever I was ready. French, however, gave me hope.

"*Hey, Jones, I heard what happened to you yesterday. Don't worry about nothing. I got you covered. You're on my payroll full-time now. Same as with my predecessor...all cash basis. You can apply for unemployment if you want. Most of my guys do, 'cause their pay is off the books. That check from Uncle Sam is like an extra benefit you can put away for retirement. No need to call. Payday is every Friday. Just see Laverne at the front desk. She'll have an envelope for you.*"

French didn't realize I was not unemployed. Officially, I was still attached to the Willow Falls PD until I was terminated or I quit. However, thanks to the Kangaroo Committee, in seven days I would not be earning any more money. If I applied for unemployment, the human resources office would tell Uncle Sam I was a duly employed member of the police department on furlough. Uncle Sam would then deny my application for unemployment benefits. I was stuck in Nowhereville, except French was making me whole, so to speak. It looked like Laverne was going to see me every Friday.

****

Against my friend Mescal's advice, a week later I drove into Albany and wandered around the warehouse district until I saw the cockfighting arena. It looked like any other warehouse, except four cars with ball fringe in their rear windows were parked in front, and the pavement beside the overflowing dumpster was littered with empty India and Corona beer cartons.

I parked my sedan and entered the unlocked door. Inside, the lights were on and two men were sweeping the grandstand and the floors around the ring. The air smelled of stale beer and sweat. One of the men said something to me in Spanish.

"Ola, señor. Donde esta Señor Prognostico?" It was broken Spanish, but I was trying.

"Señor Prognostico?"

"Si."

The guy dropped the handle of his broom against his chest and pointed toward the back area, where Mescal and I had prepped his rooster Diablo to fight in the arena last fall. I waved a "thank you" and found my way to the prepping area. When I opened the door, two men were sitting at a folding picnic table, pulling dollar bills from a wooden box and laying them in neat stacks. When the door squeaked as it closed behind me, they both looked up in surprise. The younger of the two lifted a revolver from the table and pointed it at me. He barked something at me in Spanish.

I raised my hands. "Ola, amigos. Habla Inglés?" Again, it was broken Spanish, but I think it got the message across. "Señor French sent me. Señor Prognostico?"

The young man put the pistol down and said something in a soft voice to the older man, who removed his dirty denim jacket and draped it over the stacks of money on the table.

"I am Señor Prognostico," the younger man said. "Come with me."

I followed him back into the arena area and then upstairs into a supply room where we could chat in private. He was as buff a man as I had seen in quite a while, probably from lifting weights and following a strict protein diet. And maybe from injecting steroids into his biceps and pectorals. He was wearing tight-fitting black stretch pants and a long sleeve white shirt which clung to his biceps and chest like it was skin.

He pointed at a chair. I sat. He pulled over a full case of tallboy Coronas and sat on top of it. "French sent you?"

I nodded.

"How can I help you?"

"My name is Jones. I'm trying to locate two of Caesar's men, one of whom worked here with you and the other who came here with him the night he disappeared."

"You're referring to Jorge Perez?"

"Yes. You're aware he has disappeared, aren't you?"

"Yes, French has already inquired about him."

"I understand Perez was a thorn in your side."

"Did Caesar say that?"

I shook my head. "No, I heard it elsewhere."

He reached for two beers on the shelf behind him, unscrewed the caps, and handed me one. It was a Modelo Negra. I had never tasted one. "They're better warm," he said.

I tasted mine. I was not sure I agreed with him, but I was always up for a free beer, even if it was room temperature.

"Jorge…he thought he owned my arena. He wanted free *cervezas* and *banano*. He bothered my help, especially the *jovencitas*."

I didn't understand what he was saying and tilted my head.

Prognostico understood my problem. "Ah, you truly are a gringo. Jorge wanted free beer and marijuana. And he bothered the young ladies who work for me. I asked Caesar to send someone else to work here, but he never did. Do I miss Jorge? Not a bit. That older man in the other room, he is Jorge's replacement. He doesn't drink and he doesn't mess with the girls. One of them is his granddaughter. *Comprendes*?"

It was an interesting solution to the problem of a womanizing collections agent who drank all the profits, but it didn't answer the question of where I would find Jorge Perez or Chico Herrera.

"You got any ideas about what happened to Perez and Herrera?"

"I've always got ideas, but if you're thinking I did something to them, you're barking up the wrong tree."

"I'm just looking for a direction to go."

Prognostico broke into a big grin. "You're Caesar's new bird dog, aren't you? I heard about you. You're the cop that got himself in trouble."

His comment was a gut shot. It seemed like everybody knew my personal business, and it was both embarrassing and hurtful.

"So, what ideas do you have about what happened to them?" I asked.

"They could be in a witness protection program. Or they could have been picked up by ICE and deported. Or they could have run off with the week's gate receipts and gotten married…"

I could see I was getting nowhere with Prognostico. In fact, he was playing with me.

"Okay, you can be funny, too. So, do you have any real suspicions or am I reporting to French that I left here with nothing useful?"

Prognostico's face became serious. "You know, Mr.

Jones, I think you're never gonna find either of those hombres. Caesar has been messing around in the business of others who don't play nice. I think those hombres of his are gone…wiped away as a message to Caesar that he should back off what he's doing."

I offered what I guessed French was involved in. "You mean construction?"

"No, I mean trash. I think whoever snatched them was after Herrera, not Perez. Jorge was just collateral damage. And the money he was carrying was just a surprise bonus."

I remembered Herrera was a trash truck driver for French's new company, Scentless Waste Removal. "You think it was Onondaga?"

"I think it was Los Cuernos."

Chapter Seven

When I returned home to Mariaville, my rural route box contained a single letter from the City of Willow Falls. I opened it before going inside my cabin. It was a note from Personnel ordering me to return my sedan and its keys to the motor pool no later than four p.m. on Thursday. Failure to do so would result in my arrest for unauthorized possession of city-owned property. I had only the weekend to get a new vehicle, or I would be hitchhiking. That prune-faced woman from Personnel was really hammering me, making it impossible for me to live or work.

I called French.

"Hey, Jones. You got news for me?"

"I don't have anything concrete yet, but I'll let you know as soon as I do. But I've got a problem. The city is making me return my car until I'm off my furlough and back at work. You got one I can borrow for a little while?"

French was silent for a few moments. "You know, I think I do. I'll tell you when I know for sure. Meanwhile, keep an eye on your text messages."

"Thanks, Mr. French."

"Call me Caesar. You do that when you talk to some of my associates, anyway. What is a name between friends?"

"I do it so they'll think I'm closer to you than I really

38

am. It helps me get information from them," I explained. "And you should feel free to call me Bart."

"Okay, Jones, I will." In the background I heard a knock on French's door and his secretary saying something, though I couldn't make out what she said. "Got to go, Jones. Keep your eye out for a text message from me."

****

Around ten o'clock on Tuesday morning my cell phone pinged. I had a text message from Caesar French:

—*Blue 1995 Bronco at PD guest space.*
Keys in ashtray. Enjoy.
C.—

I dressed for February weather and drove to the Willow Falls Police Department. Sitting out in front was a blue Bronco, as French had promised. I wanted to give him a big kiss. Well, not really. But he had saved my butt again. I knew someday I would have to repay him for his kindness, and that bothered me a lot. But for now, I had a nicer set of wheels than the tan sedan the city had provided for my investigative work.

I pulled up beside the Bronco, got out, and gave it the onceover. The deep lugged tires appeared new and prepared for off-roading or driving on snow. It was an automatic, so I would not have to deal with the messy gear-shifting that sometimes was inbred in older vehicles. There was some Bondo repair along the bottoms of the rear quarter panels, but the repair had been done nicely and nobody would know without knocking on the quarter panels to hear the difference between steel and Bondo. Inside, the seats were all original, but the radio had been upgraded to something more modern. I wondered if it had GPS but figured it probably didn't. I could always use my cell phone for that.

I got back into my sedan and drove it around back, where I parked in front of the small motor pool office. I walked through the damp air of the underground garage, turned in my keys, and asked for a written receipt for the return of the car. Then rather than enter the department, I walked around the building in the blustery cold to my new Bronco. The brisk air cut into my cheeks, but I felt a sense of satisfaction that the woman from Personnel had not been able to humiliate me any further.

I climbed into the Bronco and started the motor. It sounded like an eight cylinder, but it was smoother than what I expected from a twenty-five-year-old truck. The registration in was the glove compartment, and it indicated Cabrillo Construction owned the vehicle. That was okay by me because I would not be responsible for obtaining insurance. Then, while the cab warmed up, I got out and opened the hood. The motor was a six cylinder from a 2019 Ford Explorer, which meant mechanical issues would be minimal. French had thought of almost everything.

On my way back to Mariaville, I stopped for a frozen pizza and a six-pack of Moosehead Lager. There is no better way to celebrate the acquisition of a new car than pizza and beer. Well, maybe it is better if you have someone to share them with.

****

I called Helen on Saturday morning and arranged to meet her for lunch at Ruby's Red Hots. "On me," I said.

When she arrived, I was sitting in the cab of my Bronco waiting for her. The rays of the winter sun heated my face as I watched her emerge from her Hyundai. She didn't notice I was there, and she went inside ahead of me. When I came through the door a minute later, I saw her wave at me from a stool at the far end of the counter. The golden hue of the grease-stained stucco walls behind her accented her jet-black hair, which she had fashioned into a small Afro. She was dressed in blue jeans with a white turtleneck and a denim vest. It was good to see her, and she looked fabulous.

"'Bout time you called me," she said, giving me a brief hug before I sat on the red vinyl stool beside her.

"Yeah, I'm sorry about that. You warned me they were coming after me and they did. I wasn't as prepared as I should have been. Maybe I should have brought an attorney, but who could afford one?"

"Where's your sedan? I didn't see it outside, and I didn't see you drive in."

"Personnel made me turn it in. They said I couldn't be driving a city car while I'm on a rip. It really pissed me off. First, they took away my ability to earn a living and then they took away my only mode of transportation. But I got new wheels."

Helen craned her neck to look outside at the parking lot. "What you driving now?"

"That blue Bronco."

"Suits you. You're kind of a cowboy, aren't you?"

I nodded.

The waitress took our orders. Helen asked for two hotdogs with mustard and meat sauce. I had the same, but I added onions. I figured I wouldn't be kissing anybody that afternoon. We both ordered diet colas.

I started the conversation. "You got any additional information on those two bozos I asked you about?"

"You mean Perez and Herrera?"

"Yeah. They still haven't turned up. I'm thinking they may be DOA somewhere. Maybe in a dumpster."

"All I know is both worked for Cabrillo Construction. Herrera was a truck driver for the corporation's new company, a garbage business they named 'Scentless,' like they can keep garbage from stinking. They have some stiff competition from Onondaga and Tri-City Trash, but their business seems to be growing."

"Yeah. Their ads say they offer six months of free trash removal if you sign up for a year's service. How's anybody going to compete against that?"

Our hotdogs arrived. Helen put a few drops of hot sauce on her first one and took a bite. "You got me hooked on this stuff, Jonesy."

I smiled at her. "What about Perez?"

"I haven't figured out what he does for the corporation, but he was employed by Cabrillo."

"Do they have any next of kin? Anyone report them as missing?"

"Only Cabrillo. They reported them missing about a week ago."

"They didn't hurry too much, did they? But I suppose they did the proper thing, reporting their employees missing."

I finished my first hotdog and took a bite of my second. "Have you looked at their bank accounts to see if there have been any transactions since their disappearance?"

"Yup." Helen pulled a folded piece of paper from her pants pocket and opened it. "Both accounts have been closed. The money was wired to two separate branches of Banco Azteca, one in Guadalajara and one in Sinaloa."

"Maybe those two guys are alive. I wonder who else had access to the accounts?"

Helen handed me the paper. "Read it for yourself."

I studied Helen's notes. Both accounts were "joint accounts" and the second person with complete access to withdraw funds was Caesar French.

"That's interesting. Maybe he was sponsoring them to become citizens or something."

"Don't be so naïve, Jonesy. He's maybe been using their accounts to launder money or to hide it from tax accountants."

"Don't be too critical of him, Helen. He hires only new Americans, refugees who have found their way to the United States. Maybe he was under some sort of agreement to wire their money home to relatives in Mexico. That kind of money would be about five years of income for a typical Mexican in a small village. It might send younger siblings to college."

"Yeah, sure. And it might be used to pay coyotes to lead other illegal Mexicans across the border."

I swallowed my last bite of hotdog and guzzled the rest of my diet cola. "Thanks for this information, Helen. It's really helpful."

"Is that it? That's all you've got for me?"

"Listen, from the department's perspective, I'm a bad boy and you don't need to be seen helping me. It could ruin your career."

Helen took my head in her hands. "Don't you be no stranger until you get to come back. We're friends to the end, through thick and thin. Come see me at my home. Take me to a movie."

I nodded, her hands still grasping my chin bones.

"Don't you forget to call," she said. "And don't forget who loves you." She planted a promising kiss on my lips. Her face contorted. "Eeewww, you've been eating onions."

Chapter Eight

The month of February ended, and March had its predictable on-and-off weather with plenty of high winds. I spent most of that time waiting to hear from the chief that a formal hearing had been set. He never answered my phone calls, so I assumed he was not interested in putting himself through the agony of a court proceeding. I did a couple of small jobs for Caesar French, investigations into the theft of small items from his workshop and one case of income tax evasion brought onto one of his junior employees by the Internal Revenue Service. I helped solve the thefts easily, and I worked with Caesar's accountant to gather enough evidence to persuade the IRS to lay off the undocumented immigrant. French was paying me twenty percent more than the department did, and my pay was cash, so no taxes came out of it. The work I did for him was not worth what I was being paid, but I didn't complain.

Meanwhile, things were heating up in the garbage business. French called me in on April tenth, five days after Easter.

"We got a problem," he said. "We lost two garbage trucks yesterday. They stole them both the same way but in different locations. They had a cop car pull the truck over, but no cop was in it. Instead, the car had four men with baseball bats. They jerked my guys out of their trucks and worked them over. Then they took the trucks and left the men on the sidewalk. Can you find out who did it?"

"Probably, if I can gain access to the warehouses at Onondaga and Tri-City Trash. Give me a couple of days. Are the drivers okay?"

"They got beaten up pretty bad, but nothing which won't heal. If it was Onondaga, they must have clamped down pretty hard on Los Cuernos because they didn't kill anybody."

I drove to Albany and found the Onondaga Disposal Company, located a block away from the county's recycling plant. I parked outside the main warehouse and walked in. A team of men was busy spray painting a black garbage truck. The Z on the driver's side door had not yet been painted. Another truck recently had been painted and was drying under strong lights and several fans.

"Hey, you! Get out of here!" The warning was issued by a tall guy with a hairy chest, wearing an orange hard hat and carrying a baseball bat.

I took two steps backward. "I want to apply for a job."

"You don't do that in here." He pointed his bat out the door. "The office is in the next building, green door. Ask for Shirley."

"Thanks, buddy."

I turned and walked back out the door.

It had been a quick investigation, with observed evidence on the location of one truck. I could not be certain the other truck was one of French's, but it probably was. And I had not been able to take a picture as hard evidence of the theft.

I wanted something to show French, so I climbed into my Bronco. I started the motor and drove into the warehouse, honking my horn and squealing my tires as my truck did a donut and came to a stop thirty feet from the trash truck which was being painted. The men inside scattered. I raised my cell phone and took two quick pictures. The sound of shattering glass erupted from behind me. I felt small particles of glass bounce off the back of my head. I hit the accelerator and peeled out of the warehouse. In my side-view mirror I could see the guy who had directed me to the main office holding his bat high in the air and yelling something unintelligible.

I made multiple turns and changed directions several times as I left Albany, hoping I would lose anyone who might have tagged along behind me. When I felt I was safe, I took back roads from Albany to Schenectady and then to Willow Falls.

French was standing outside his office when I arrived. He was either coming from or going to a meeting somewhere. Maybe he had just returned from lunch.

"Hey, Jones." He put his hand on his forehead. "What did you do to my truck?"

"The rear window is compliments of Onondaga Trash," I said as I got out of the Bronco. "I guess I got too close to the guy with the baseball bat."

French reached behind my head and picked a few pieces of broken glass from my shoulders. "You learn anything else while you were there?"

"Yeah." I opened my cell phone and showed him the two pictures I had taken. One was blurry, but the other showed the Scentless logo on a truck being painted with Onondaga's green and yellow.

"Bastards," French snapped. "What about Tri-

City?"

"I'm heading to Troy now. I should know something by tomorrow."

"Good. But try not to ruin my Bronco in the process. Tomorrow morning take it to Willow Falls Glass and have the rear window replaced. Have them send me the bill. I'll forward it to my insurance company."

In ten minutes, I was on my way to Troy, home of nationally famous Uncle Sam and known as the "Collar City" to truck drivers. It was a forty-minute drive from Willow Falls, but I stopped for a burger and fries "to go" at a family dive along the way, so it took a little over an hour to reach Troy. Built on the side of a hill and bordered by the Hudson River, Troy offers some nice eateries, but most residences are run down, and kids play in the streets. Kids in uppity Marshfield call Troy kids "Troylets." That should say enough.

I found Tri-City Trash along the river, where local garbage is unloaded from trucks onto barges which then drift down the Hudson River and out to sea just north of New Jersey. There, they are dumped, and Troy's paper, plastic, and medical waste finds its way to the coastlines and beaches of New Jersey and Delaware. Sweet, huh?

Tri-City Trash was located in a series of rusty steel buildings in Troy's "warehouse row." Their trucks were lined up outside, all painted in light brown and orange with the Tri-City logo emblazoned on their sides in dark brown. Several men were hosing road dirt off them from the daily runs around the capital region.

I tried the same approach as I had at Onondaga. I entered a building where activity was ongoing and asked where I could apply for work.

The first two men I asked just shrugged their

shoulders. They were probably immigrants, but I was not sure from which countries. Obviously, they could not understand what I asked, but they were not bothered by my unexpected arrival. One wore a shirt with a blue flag on it. A white stripe crossed the flag at its middle, and a circular national symbol was printed in black, but I did not get close enough to read it.

Eventually, I found a guy who spoke broken English.

"Where can I apply for a job?" I asked.

"See Jose." He pointed at the next building.

"Do you guys paint trucks here?"

"Utica."

I nodded. "Thank you very much."

I climbed back into my Bronco and drove home. Tri-City did not seem a likely place to find a Scentless truck being painted. Maybe I would travel to Utica, but it seemed like a fruitless task, especially since I had seen two trucks being painted at Onondaga's warehouse in Albany. And French had only two stolen.

When I returned, I told French I didn't see anything out of the ordinary at Tri-City. He didn't seem surprised.

"Their trucks are painted in Utica, so maybe I'll head over there tomorrow and see what I can find out. Meanwhile, can you tell me which country has a blue flag with a white stripe down its middle?"

"El Salvador, Jones. You got to learn something about the homelands of your new American neighbors."

"Isn't El Salvador the home of MS-13?"

"No, I think Mara Salvatrucha started in L.A., but it was started by Salvadorians. Like Los Cuernos, they use violence to control neighborhoods."

The next morning I drove to Willow Falls glass and

sat in the waiting room while the technicians installed new glass where my rear window used to be. Then, at eleven, I drove to Utica and checked out Tri-City Trash. Its offices were located a mile from the Thruway on Leland Avenue, which ran between Incinerator Street and Sewage Plant Road. The names of the streets aptly described the environs. It was another run-down section of a river town, not unlike Troy.

I drove through the open gate of an eight-foot-tall chain-link fence, and then circled the three warehouses as though I belonged there. Doors were open at both ends of all three buildings, letting the warmer spring air inside. I saw no painting going on, and I saw no freshly painted trucks. Instead, the six I did see were lined up between two buildings and were banged up and rusty. They were probably awaiting scheduled repairs and fresh paint jobs.

Chapter Nine

On Saturday, I visited Oates Feed and Supply Store in the Town of Schoharie to find a mousetrap to rid my cabin of two pesky critters I had seen run along the wall under my kitchen table. I was amazed at the variety of traps I could choose from, everything from traditional spring traps to plastic gizmos that snap down on unsuspecting mice like the open jaws of a white shark. Then, of course, were "bring 'em back alive" traps that captured mice unharmed in little cages so you could relocate them to your backyard and catch them again the next day.

Several other customers were rummaging around inside, too. My attention was drawn to an old woman who was drifting through the aisles as though she had never been there before. Occasionally she would pick up a small item, inspect it closely, and then put it back on its shelf, muttering a few words about price and value. She was dressed in a long cotton sleeveless dress, purple with yellow sunflowers printed just above the hemline. Her veined calves were shaped like rounded four by fours from her hemline to her white socks, which were rolled at her ankles where they squeezed into low-cut brown working shoes.

The woman finally picked up a bag of weed killer and brought it to the front counter. Mr. Gartshore, the store owner, peered over his semicircular reading glasses as she placed it down firmly. White dust puffed from the bag's folded top. The woman brushed it off her hands and wrists.

"Can't they ever find a way to keep dust in the bag where it belongs?" she asked.

Gartshore shook his head in agreement. "Things just aren't the same as they used to be, are they?"

"Got to get ahead of those damned weeds. Summer's coming and the heat will bring the Canadian thistles back to life…and the milkweed and the poison ivy, as well."

Gartshore shook his head again. He studied the price tag and tapped the keys on his cash register. "That'll be twelve seventy-six."

I selected a four-pack of traditional snap traps, walked up behind a man who was second in line behind the old woman and waited my turn.

The old woman plopped her two-gallon cloth purse on the counter, opened it, and began searching for her wallet. "Heat's gotten so bad you can't get good help anymore. Used to be people wanted to work, but not anymore. I hired a Mexican man to help me last fall. He raked and burned a lot of leaves. He was supposed to come back and help me with the lawn and the weeding this spring, but he never showed up."

"That will be twelve seventy-six," Gartshore repeated.

"Hold your darn horses." She fished around in her purse some more, pulled out a red wallet, and counted out twelve one-dollar bills. Then she unzipped the coin compartment and retrieved three quarters and one penny. She handed them to Gartshore. "Know any kids who want to work for college money?"

"Nosiree," he said. "But thank you for your purchase and have a nice day."

The old woman stood firmly in place. "You're darn right about that. They don't want to work. They don't believe in self-sufficiency. They expect the government will give them free college." She put the straps of her purse over her shoulder. As she turned to leave, she muttered, "They'd better learn how to work and save money with prices like these. Can you believe a bag of basic weed killer now costs over twelve dollars? When I was younger, you could feed a family of four on twelve dollars a week."

"Good afternoon, ma'am," Gartshore said. Then he turned to the man who was next in line. "Did you find everything you needed?"

The man plopped a pipe wrench and a tube of plumber's putty on the counter. "Who is that old biddy, Mr. Gartshore?" he whispered. "She's as caustic a person as I've ever seen."

"You ain't kidding. That's Mrs. Malbrook. Lives out on Mariaville Lake. I think she drinks battery acid for breakfast. Not got much nice to say about anybody. For certain, nobody's got nothing nice to say about her."

"I've heard rumors about Mrs. Malbrook. They say she eats weeds."

"Could be. She don't buy much food from me, 'ceptin' oil and butter and milk. I think she pretty much lives off the land, you know…supplementing her chickens and her garden with wild plants and berries. She's a bitter old hen."

****

At seven thirty in the morning, Mrs. Malbrook hurried to the Faulkner's cabin. Her grey hair was barely combed, and her low-top slip-on sneakers were wet from the morning dew. She knocked loudly on the screen door.

Mr. Faulkner came to the door holding a cup of coffee. He was in his sleeping briefs and a white tee shirt. "Good morning, neighbor."

Mrs. Malbrook's expression showed serious concern. "You need to come with me. It's something awful."

Twelve-year-old Emma pushed past her father. Her straw-colored braids were coming apart. "Good morning, Mrs. Malbrook. Want some toast?"

"No thank you, sweetheart. But your daddy needs to put his boots on and come with me."

"Can I come, too, Daddy?" Emma pleaded.

"No, darling," Mrs. Malbrook said. "It's not something for you to see."

Mr. Faulkner gently nudged his daughter from the door. "Go eat your cereal, Emma." He returned his attention to his visitor. "Would you like to come in, Mrs. Malbrook?"

"Thank you, but my shoes are already muddy, and I don't want to cause your wife any work. I'll wait out here."

Mr. Faulkner closed the door and went to his bedroom.

Mrs. Faulkner rose to her elbow on the mattress. "Who was at the door, Marvin?"

Mr. Faulkner quickly put on jeans. Then he rummaged through the pile of shoes on the closet floor and retrieved his boots. His sweat socks were stuffed into them. He sat down on the bed. "It's Mrs. Malbrook. She's waiting outside for me. Wants me to see something in the woods. I'll be back in a few minutes."

He laced his boots, put on his blue spring-weight jacket and joined Mrs. Malbrook outside. As they walked into the woods, he asked, "What is so upsetting, Mrs. Malbrook?"

"It's a man's body, Mr. Faulkner. Wait until you see it."

They climbed for seventy or eighty yards, the angle of the wooded hill increasing as they proceeded. Twice Mrs. Malbrook asked to take a short pause to catch her breath.

They approached an area where the damp brown leaves of the forest floor had been disturbed, Mrs. Malbrook stopped and pointed at a small heap of leaves. "It's right over there,"

Mr. Faulkner stepped closer to take a look. "Ugh," he said. "Thank you for not letting Emma come along."

"It's a man's body, isn't it?" Mrs. Malbrook asked.

"Yes, I think it is…what's left of it." He pointed at torn and bloody blue jeans and work boots. "Those items look like something a man would wear."

"Well, lots of women wear denims and boots up here, too."

"The body is a mess."

"Did you hear the commotion last night? I'll bet he was eaten by a bear."

Mr. Faulkner nodded.

"You keep Emma inside at night, you hear? Once he's got a taste of human blood, the bear might want more."

Mr. Faulkner found a broken branch and poked it at the remains, not sure what he would find.

Meanwhile, Mrs. Malbrook found a stick of her own

and prodded at the torn clothing. As she turned one swatch, a rectangle of dark brown leather fell onto the wet leaves. "I found a wallet."

Mr. Faulkner joined her, picked up the wallet and opened it. "All the money and credit cards are gone, but the driver's license is here. His name is Jorge Perez."

"Land sakes, that's what happened to him. He was my Mexican worker last fall. No wonder he didn't come back to work this spring. Maybe he came back for lunch one day but didn't know he was going to be the main course."

Mrs. Malbrook's wry humor escaped Mr. Faulkner. "We probably ought to call the police."

Back at Mrs. Malbrook's cabin, Mr. Faulkner dialed the number while Mrs. Malbrook recited it to him from a penciled note she had made on her door jamb, and then he set his cell phone on the "speaker" option. They heard a recorded message:

"The police department is closed today. If this is an emergency, call the New York State Police."

Next, they dialed the State Police, as directed.

"We have a possible animal attack which has resulted in a human death," Mr. Faulkner said to the officer who answered. "We tried the Duanesburg Police, but they're closed today."

"They aren't equipped to handle a homicide, anyway," the officer said.

Twenty minutes later, three squad cars of New York State Police answered the call. One car brought two dogs, a German shepherd and a bloodhound.

When Emma saw them from the kitchen window, she wanted to go pet the dogs, but her mom would not let her out of the house. "They're working dogs, honey.

They have a job to do, and you don't want to be in their way."

Mrs. Malbrook and Mr. Faulkner both gave verbal reports to the State Police, and then stayed behind while the police did their work. An hour later a trooper knocked on Mrs. Malbrook's back door.

"We got the body, Ma'am," he said. "Another squad found the decomposed head in the ditch on the other side of the road up above. Thank you for reporting what you found. You shouldn't have touched the wallet, but given how long it's been outside, I imagine any prints are long gone."

Next door, Mr. Faulkner told his wife and daughter what Mrs. Malbrook had discovered. "A ranger was with them, ENCON I believe. He told me the body probably had been dumped there from the road during the winter. It stayed frozen until a bear discovered it and pulled it down the mountainside to eat it."

"Do bears really eat humans, Marvin?" Mrs. Faulkner asked.

"No, they're not supposed to. According to the ranger, bears don't usually eat humans, but the bears have been hibernating all winter and have lost over a hundred pounds of weight. When they wake up, they're ravenous. This time of year, they feed on recent roadkill and baby animals, like fawns and baby rabbits. The bear probably thought the man was roadkill."

Chapter Ten

As I was about to take New York State Thruway Exit Twenty-five toward Mariaville, my cell phone rang. It was Helen. It is against the law to use a cell phone while operating a motor vehicle, but like thousands of scofflaws, I punched the answer button with my thumb and did anyway.

"Hello, ladybug," I said warmly.

"You never call me anymore, Jonesy."

She was right about that. "I'm sorry. I've just been busy with little things while I'm waiting for the chief to schedule my hearing. The weather is nice though. What's up?"

"You know those two guys you were looking for?"

I thought for a moment. "Oh, you mean Perez and Herrera?"

"Yeah. Well one of them just turned up in your back yard."

"My back yard? It was a plant! I wouldn't leave a dead body in my back yard."

"Cut it out, you jerk. Perez's body, or what was left of it, showed up on the other side of Mariaville Lake from you."

"Really? How's the body? Probably badly decomposed?"

"It's mostly skin and bones. Probably spent the winter frozen in a snowbank, and then it looks like a bear found it and has been eating it for several days."

"How do they know it was Perez?

"His wallet was found in the shredded clothes." Helen paused a moment. I could tell she was thinking. "Rough place out there where you live, especially if a bear maybe is gonna eat you for dinner."

"Where's the body now?"

"Medical Examiner's. I'll get some more details for you later. Chief is putting me on the case. Maybe we can share information."

"That sounds good, Helen. It'll be nice working with you again. Thanks."

After Helen hung up, I pulled off the road onto a wide strip of shoulder and called French.

"Hello, Jones. What did you learn in Utica?"

"I think Utica was a wasted trip. The only trucks out there are Tri-City trucks, and all of them are badly in need of repair and painting."

"Then the trip was not wasted. We need to focus on Onondaga…reclaim our property."

"I've got more news for you. You'll probably hear from the Willow Falls Police soon. Perez's body was found in the woods on the western side of Mariaville Lake this morning."

"Out where you live?"

"Yeah. His body was decapitated. Whoever did it threw his head on one side of the road and his body on the other side. The cops think a bear found the corpse in a snowbank and has been feeding on it for several days."

"How do they know it was Perez?

"They found his wallet. It's always possible the body is somebody else and the killer put Perez's wallet on the body to throw investigators off track. I mean, like

Perez could have killed somebody himself and put his own wallet on the body to throw the cops off. But I think it's unlikely."

I waited for him to process what I had told him. French was silent for half a minute. I knew he cared greatly for his men, and this news was not good. Eventually he spoke. "Is there any word on Herrera?"

"No, nothing yet, but I'll keep working on it."

I heard French blow his nose. Clearly, the news about Perez had evoked an emotional response. "Back to Jorge," he said. "How was his head decapitated?"

"I don't know. The body is with the medical examiner right now. The police might call you before I get any further information, but I'll call you the moment I have more details."

"If it was severed by a machete, then it was Los Cuernos. Onondaga has fired the first shot by stealing my trucks, and perhaps they killed the first victim. War already may have begun, and I didn't even realize it."

French hung up the phone.

I drove back to Mariaville.

Helen called again at four in the afternoon.

"Hey, Helen. I didn't expect to hear from you again until tomorrow."

"The medical examiner has finished his report. So, I have a few more tidbits for you. Doc says the head was chopped off, either by an axe or a machete. Given the narrow width of the gashes, he thinks it was most likely a machete. Victim's been dead several months. Given the amount of road salt in the hair on the head, Doc agrees the body lay frozen in the snow until some animal found it during the spring thaw. Doc agrees it was probably a bear."

French was right. Los Cuernos probably killed Perez. I wondered if we would ever find Herrera's body. Meanwhile, it appeared the war everyone feared was imminent had already begun. I wondered how French would retaliate.

"You still there, Jonesy?"

"Yeah," I replied. "Doc seems agreeable today."

"The ENCON bear specialist concurs the bear probably dragged the body away from the road to feed on it. He believes the bear covered it with leaves each time he finished feeding, so birds and coyotes would leave the carcass alone."

It was interesting the State Police would call in a specialist from the NY Department of Environmental Conservation. I would have to learn more about that. Meanwhile, I wanted to see the site where the body was found. The state Police might have failed to discover everything.

"Would you happen to have the name of the person who found the body or the location of the discovery?"

"I assumed you would want that. It's Mrs. Naomi Malbrook. She's in her early eighties. I'm going out to see her tomorrow morning. You want to tag along?"

I remembered Mrs. Malbrook from the feed and seed store in Schoharie. She was the "weed-eater."

"Sure. What time are you picking me up?"

"About ten. That way she's had time to straighten her home and take a shower. I think you should follow her example."

"You mean straighten my house, too?"

"Yeah. You got a female coming to see where you live. You gonna let her see what a pig you are?"

Helen had a point.

****

Helen pulled into the extra parking space at my cabin at exactly ten o'clock in the morning. I waved from the door and then picked up my notebook and joined her in her Hyundai.

"Cute little place," she said. "Kind of like Daniel Boone meets Davy Crockett."

"I cleaned it, just in case you wanted to see the inside."

Helen smiled smugly. "Good. It probably needed a major cleaning. I'm glad my little talk got you off your ass and doing something positive for yourself."

She pulled out of my driveway and then headed to the main road, a paved two-lane strip of asphalt which wound from Schenectady to Cobleskill and beyond. We crossed the Mariaville bridge and took a right turn about two hundred yards on the other side. Half a mile down the gravel road, Helen stopped. She reached into her jacket pocket and pulled out a card. "It's the third mailbox, number 82-B." She turned onto the driveway, which bent to the left for one hundred yards before ending at a small gray lakefront cabin.

"Yes, this is it. She should be waiting for us."

We got out and walked around to the front of the house. Helen knocked on the sliding glass door. While we waited for a response, I turned toward the lake and spotted my cabin across the water. If Mrs. Malbrook and I stood on our respective docks, we could wave at each other in the light of day.

Mrs. Malbrook struggled to slide her glass door open. "Thought you folks would be coming to my back door. Don't get too many folks coming to this side of my house."

"Hello, Mrs. Malbrook," Helen said. "I'm Detective Helen Martin. The gentleman with me is Bart Jones."

"I'm representing the firm which first reported Mr. Perez as a missing person," I said.

Mrs. Malbrook shook our hands. "I suppose you'd like to see where we found the body?"

"Yes, please," Helen replied.

Mrs. Malbrook stepped outside. She was wearing loose-fitting khaki pants, a yellow "Mariaville Lake" tee shirt, and a lightweight unzipped green sweatshirt. Her gray hair was tucked under a New England Patriots baseball cap.

We followed her up a gentle slope, but it soon became not so gentle. She stopped to let me catch my breath. Twice. Finally, we reached the site. Yellow crime scene tape was still strung in a semi-square shape between four tree trunks. The ground had been well-trampled by the State's investigators.

"I understand you knew the victim," Helen said.

"Yes, Mr. Perez worked for me as a gardener and general handyman last fall. He helped me pull and burn weeds, bring in my dock, and mow my property. You know…it needed to be prepped for winter and I'm just too old to do it all by myself. He was supposed to come back for spring cleanup on April first, but he never showed up. I thought perhaps he was deported."

"You knew he was undocumented?" I asked.

"Yes. He was very up front with me about it. He said he was working to earn enough money to bring his family here. He wanted to become a citizen. I paid him ten dollars an hour in cash and tipped him fifty dollars after his week of work."

"Looks like the State Police did a good job of

cleanup," Helen said.

"Do you think they'll come back for the dern yellow tape?" Mrs. Malbrook asked. "I don't want to have to come back up here and cut it down by myself. No telling when that bear might come back."

I pulled out my pocketknife and cut the ribbon, then rolled it into a ball the size of a cantaloupe. "They probably have everything they need. If they give you any trouble about this, have them call me."

Helen gave me a look of disapproval, but she didn't say anything to negate the wisdom of my actions. However, I could tell she would have left the plastic tape there until someone from the State Police removed it.

"Can you think of anyone who might have wanted to hurt Mr. Perez?" she asked.

"No, not at all," Mrs. Malbrook replied.

"Did he mention if he had any problems with anybody…his boss, an acquaintance, a woman?"

"Nope. Like I said, he was a hard worker."

Helen and I walked back down to Mrs. Malbrook's cabin with her. She took off her sweatshirt and laid it on her small deck. She picked up a garden rake and started walking toward her waterfront. Then she stopped and turned. "You wouldn't happen to know anybody who'd like a job pulling weeds would you?"

Helen looked at me and nodded in Mrs. Malbrook's direction. "Couldn't you use a few extra bucks?"

"I'll see if I can find someone to help you, Ma'am," I said. There was no way I was pulling weeds for anybody. My mother made me hate weed pulling when she forced me to do it in her flower beds as a kid. It was hot, dirty work, and nobody could pay me enough to do it as an adult.

Helen drove me home, a quick five minutes away.

I offered her a chance to see my digs. "Come on in and let me give you something to drink."

"I can stay for only a minute or two. There's stuff to do back at the office."

I opened the door so she could go in first. I had busied myself in the morning cleaning house so it would not look too bad for Helen. The air inside smelled like the bleach I had left in the toilet bowl.

"Aren't you renting this place from Joey Astor?" she asked. "I thought he had plans for it this summer. When does he want you out?"

"His plans have changed. I can stay for another twelve months, but he's bumped the rent up to two hundred fifty dollars per month."

"Can you afford it?"

"Yeah, most certainly." These accommodations were just fine for a single man, and I was happy to have them. Joey had let me stay rent free over the winter, but in April he had asked for two hundred fifty dollars per month beginning in May. Where could a guy rent a lake-front two-bedroom house for that kind of money?

Helen walked into my bedroom and then into my guest room, looking at everything.

"You didn't decorate this place yourself, did you?"

I laughed. "No, it came furnished like this. I may make some changes this summer. The bed could use a new mattress and the living room furniture is from the nineteen fifties."

"I noticed."

Helen walked to my sliding glass door and stared across the lake. "Isn't that Mrs. Malbrook's place right over there?"

I stood beside her and peered across the lake. "Yeah, I guess it is."

"That old lady could use some help, Jonesy. I hope you were serious about finding her some. You've got spare time, don't you?"

I didn't answer her. If I had, I would have been making a commitment to help an old lady who seemed fairly strong to me. Well, strong enough to pull all the weeds from her waterfront by herself if she kept at it slowly and took breaks. I changed the subject. "Do you have any more information for me about Perez?"

"Nothing you don't already suspect. State labs found bear saliva on the bones, and they agree his head was severed by a machete, chopped like you would a tree branch, probably after he died. No signs of toxins in his blood. Road salt was on everything."

Chapter Eleven

It was uncharacteristic of me, but the next morning I dressed in shorts and drove over to Mrs. Malbrook's. I re-introduced myself and helped her pull weeds from the water beside her dock. We would each grab a handful and plop them on an old green tarp she had laid on the graying boards of her dock. We had been working for about thirty minutes when a little girl showed up on her dock, making the old nails and boards creak as she walked toward us.

"Hi, Mrs. Malbrook. Do you need any more help?"

"Emma, this is Mr. Jones. Mr. Jones, this is Emma Faulkner. Her family rents the cabin next door every summer."

"My real name is Emma Rose Faulkner."

I looked up. Emma Rose stood about four and a half feet tall. She was wearing tan overalls with short bottoms, perhaps altered by her mother, and a pink tee shirt. The toes of her sneakers were already wet from walking across the dew-soaked grass.

"Well, hello, Emma Rose," I said. "Are you here to help?"

"Emma likes to drag the tarp with the weeds over to my fire pit," Mrs. Malbrook said. "While she's about her business, I usually take a two-minute break." She squinted in the sunlight as she looked up at Emma. If you're ready, this tarp is probably over-full. Think you can manage it by yourself?"

Emma picked up the end of the tarp and began dragging it across the boards of the dock. "I'll get it, but it would help if you wouldn't put so many weeds on next time."

"Okay, honey," Mrs. Malbrook called out to her. She looked at me. "That girl's a hustler. She's going to make something of herself. Probably drive her husband crazy trying to keep up with her."

"Do you do this kind of work every day?"

"Yessiree. If I don't, the weeds take over. I pull lake weeds two hours each day…water chestnuts, milfoil, and run-of-the-mill lake weeds. On Monday I start by the bank on the left side of the dock and work my way toward the deep water at the end. On Thursday I start on the right side of the dock and work my way back toward the shoreline."

"It's incredible they grow so fast. Pulling them has to tire you out pretty fast."

"Yes, it does. But then after lunch I pull weeds and spread bug killer on the plants in my vegetable garden and on the decorative gardens around the house."

My cell phone rang. I had forgotten to take it out of my shorts pocket. Fortunately, we had not gotten into deep water yet, so water had not found its way to my phone.

"Excuse me, Naomi," I said. "It's a work call."

The call was coming from Cabrillo Construction. It was probably French.

"Bart Jones." I said into the phone.

"We got problems, Jones."

Yup, it was French. "Hi, Caesar. How can I help?"

"We lost another truck this morning. I've got to

respond to these thefts. Can you come in immediately?"

"How's the driver?"

"His name is Sung-Ho Sin. He was beaten severely. Broken ribs and nose. He's in the hospital, but he'll live. I've asked the minister of the Korean Presbyterian Church to stop in to comfort him."

"At least that's good. Would you like me to see if the truck is being painted at Onondaga before I come in?"

"No. I've sent one of my men to check it out. He should be back soon."

I needed to go home and change my clothes before I drove to Cabrillo Construction. "Okay, I'll be there in forty-five minutes."

Naomi looked at me, disappointed that I would be leaving. "Will you come back another day, Bart?"

"You can count on it. Maybe together we can get ahead of these weeds, and you can take a day off."

Emma Rose was dragging the empty tarp onto the dock as I walked out of the water. "Are you leaving, mister?"

"Unfortunately, yes. I have to go to work for a while. You be sure to keep helping Mrs. Malbrook. She needs all the help she can get."

"Sure will. She pulls them and I drag them. On Saturdays we burn them."

I patted the dock near her feet. "See you next time, Emma Rose."

****

I arrived at Cabrillo Construction at eleven in the morning. Laverne told me French was in the warehouse talking with his men. I walked through the hallway and onto the warehouse's concrete floor just as a dozen men were leaving, several of them armed with AK-47s.

"Hey, Jones," French said when he saw me.

"What's up with all the men, and why the firepower?"

He put his hand on my shoulder and turned me back toward his office. "They're going to get my trucks back."

This news sounded ominous to me. "How will you know which ones are yours? They've all been painted."

"They took three, so I'm taking three back. Onondaga isn't the only business with a paint shop. The three we take will be Scentless trucks by midnight."

"Aren't you afraid of starting a war?"

The sound of squealing tires drew our attention to the asphalt area outside the warehouse. Several men shouted. Tires squealed again. A moment later, one of French's men came running into the warehouse and hurried up to him, rapidly spewing something to him in Spanish.

French opened his hand, and the man carefully placed a balled-up handkerchief into it. French opened the handkerchief. It contained a bloody finger with a silver ring. The letter U had been tattooed in dark blue on the top of the largest section of the finger.

"Oh my god," he whispered. He looked at the man who had carried the finger. "Muñoz?"

"Si, señor."

French said something else to the man, who then turned and hurried back outside, the back of his shirt stained in a V from sweat.

French looked at me. His eyes were watering. "As I told you the other day, the war has begun, and another of our soldiers has fallen."

"Was Muñoz the guy you sent to spy on

Onondaga?"

"Yes, Manuel Muñoz."

We walked into his office, where he placed the finger into a cigar box which was on the shelf behind his desk.

"Sit, Jones."

I took my usual seat across the desk from French. He looked at me with sadness in his eyes. "It is going to be like New Jersey...death behind every door. I truly didn't want this."

"Nobody wants a real war between competing businesses, especially the people of the capital region of New York. They won't be able to comprehend the violence."

French nodded. "So, what do I do? I cannot let my men fall prey to more violence without revenge."

"First, you send me to do the snooping. I'm a trained investigator. Second, you never send one of your men out on the road alone. You always send someone to ride shotgun, especially in your trash trucks...someone armed with one of your AKs. And your driver should always have a pistol in his belt."

"That's good advice. I will do as you suggest."

"And you might want to think twice about stealing Onondaga's trucks. Get your new ones from out of state."

"It is too late for that. My men have already begun their mission. The trucks will be here and ready to paint before the end of the day."

"Then put two armed guards at every corner of your property, two armed guards inside every building, and secure your gates with barriers at all times...twenty-four-seven."

French nodded.

"And put some sandbags in the window where Laverne sits. She's an easy target."

The sound of a large truck entering the warehouse and squealing to a stop interrupted our conversation. French leaped to his feet and left the office. I followed closely behind him. As we entered the warehouse, we could see one squad of his men had done their work quickly. The driver was climbing out of an Onondaga truck. Dirty water was dripping onto the warehouse floor from the truck's trash compacting cell.

"Close the damn door," French shouted. One of the men quickly closed the large warehouse door. Then French spoke with the driver of the truck. The man smiled and said something I couldn't hear. French nodded.

He stepped over to me. "This truck was spotted only a dozen blocks away. The Onondaga driver was armed and resisted, so they had to kill him. He is in with the trash."

I nodded, not knowing what else to say. I was observing the acts of war between men representing half a dozen third-world countries. I needed to remain as uninvolved as possible, but I knew I could easily be swept up into the conflict. And I knew it was going to get messy quickly.

Chapter Twelve

My phone rang at two in the morning. I found it on my nightstand and unplugged the charger cord. It was Helen. "You okay?" I asked, forgetting to say, "Hello."

"I'm checking on you. Things in Schenectady have gone bonkers tonight. Sirens all over the place. Chief called to alert me to the possibility that some of the trouble could spill over into Willow Falls or even Glen Cove."

The floor felt cold to my feet as I sat up on the edge of my bed. "Really? What kind of trouble?"

"Someone is setting trash cans on fire…those large plastic ones with flip lids. More than a hundred have been burned in Schenectady tonight. The fire department is at its wits end trying to extinguish them and prevent the fires from damaging trees, cars, and telephone poles."

"Really? Does the chief suspect kids?"

"No, he thinks it might be gang-related, especially since the fires have been started with some type of accelerant. And the only trash cans which have been torched have been Scentless cans."

I tried to pretend I didn't know what was going on, but there was no doubt Onondaga and their Los Cuernos soldiers were taking revenge upon French and the Scentless Waste Removal Company. The war was already entering its second inning.

"That's not good," I said. "Sounds to me like one of the other trash companies might be behind tonight's fires."

Helen's voice sounded suspicious. "Do you know something you're not telling me?"

"Nope. I'm just putting two and two together. Doesn't it make sense if only one company's trashcans are being torched, the perpetrator somehow is going to be connected to another trash company which stands to benefit from the other's bad luck? Scentless is the company which has been offering free trash removal for six months to anyone who would sign up for a year's service. The other companies have lost tons of their customers. It seems plausible one or more of the other companies is taking out revenge on Scentless Waste Removal."

Helen snorted. "You may be right, Jonesy. Sometimes you're smarter than you look. I'll have to suggest your scenario to the chief, but I won't tell him it's coming from you, okay?"

"Yeah. Don't give me any credit if you want to keep your job. And don't hesitate to call me again at this time of night. I love getting jolted out of a deep sleep."

"Good night, Jonesy."

I plugged the charger cord back into my phone and rolled back onto my mattress. I had just fallen back to sleep when my cell phone rang again. I found it in the dark and sat up on the edge of my bed again. This time it was French.

"Good morning, Caesar. I heard about your trashcans."

"Then you know?"

"Yeah, I got a call from a friend in the police

department. She says you've lost a lot of trashcans."

"Yeah, they're all melted onto the streets and into some people's yards. They even burned the one at my home." He paused. "It's going to be a difficult job to clean everything up."

"Make the city pay for it. You didn't burn your own trashcans, so you shouldn't have to pay to clean up the mess."

"Good idea, Jones. I like the way you think. I'll get my attorney on it in the morning. But this is going to ruin my business for a while."

"How long will it take to get new trashcans out to your customers who lost them?"

"I have maybe seventy on hand. I'll have to order more in the morning and get them shipped overnight."

"That's going to cost you, but you have no other choice. I assume you have insurance?"

"Of course. That is only good business. But Onondaga is going to pay, Jones. One way or another."

"Do you want me to come in? I can check how you've begun to fortify and defend your property."

"Yeah. Maybe after lunch tomorrow?"

"Okay. See you then."

Once again, I reconnected my phone to its charger cord and tried to go back to sleep. As I was drifting away, my cell phone went off for a third time. I sat up in frustration and looked at it. The telephone number was somewhat familiar, but I couldn't place it.

"Hello, Bart Jones."

"Sorry to wake you, Bart. It's Naomi Malbrook."

"Hi, Naomi. It's no problem. You may find this hard to believe, but I had just gotten off the phone. What's up?"

Her voice sounded nervous, perhaps upset. "The bear is back."

"The one who ate Mr. Perez?"

"Yes, I think so. He's grunting and huffing something awful tonight. I already went outside to try and see what the commotion is about, but I won't go into the woods after dark. Not after finding Mr. Perez."

"If you'd like, I can come over now."

"No, that shouldn't be necessary. Mr. Faulkner came outside when he heard the noise, too. We decided we shouldn't go into the woods until there's plenty of sunlight and old brother bruin has gone back to bed. I told him I'd call you so we could make it a threesome."

"Sure. What time do you want me there?"

"Maybe seven thirty?"

God, it sounded so early. "Sure. I'll be there then."

I set my phone alarm for six thirty and went back to sleep.

****

At seven thirty-five I pulled into Naomi's driveway. Better late than never. She was standing between her house and the cabin next door holding a commercially manufactured walking stick. I parked and got out.

"Good morning," I said. "Were you able to get any sleep last night?"

"Some, but not enough. That old bear was making noise for more than an hour. He kept the Faulkners up, too. Little Emma Rose didn't fall asleep until almost four."

The screen door of the house next door opened. The thin man who came out was dressed in blue jeans and a long sleeve tee shirt. He stuck out his hand. "Hi, I'm Marv Faulkner. I rent this place from Ted Landry."

"Hi, Marv. I'm Bart Jones, private investigator. I heard you've had some problems with a bear this Spring."

"I had hoped it was over, but he must live nearby. I'd like to enjoy evening campfires with my family, but with that fella roaming around I've been reluctant. He kept us up pretty late last night."

"Well, you two lead. You have a better idea of where we're going than I do."

Naomi Malbrook took the lead, with Marv close behind. I hugged close to Marv.

"I suggest we not talk until we find something," Naomi said.

"Good idea, especially if that old bear is still around," Marv said.

I disagreed. "Wouldn't it be better to make noise, so he'll beat feet if he hears us coming?"

"Let's move quietly," Naomi insisted.

We climbed slowly up the slope through the thick green leaves of springtime. The day was going to be hot and humid, and I could feel beads of sweat forming on my forehead.

Naomi stopped, not more than fifty yards from the edge of the woods. She pointed with her walking stick. "There."

I looked in the direction she had pointed and saw a pile of dark brown leaves. A hand was protruding from the pile.

"You go look," Naomi said. "I've seen one dead man and that's enough for a lifetime."

Marv and I approached the pile of leaves.

"Bear covered him up nicely," Marv said. "Keeps the sun from spoiling the meat."

I nodded, and then I bent over to inspect the hand. Its ring finger was missing. Beginning with the pinkie, each finger and the thumb had been tattooed with a letter: M-_-N-O-Z. It was Muñoz, the man whom French had sent to spy on Onondaga.

Marv found a large fallen limb and pried at the chest area, trying to roll the body over. I brushed away a handful of leaves and found the man's boots. I lifted them and flipped them as Marv pried. The body fell onto its back.

I fell back in disgust. The man's intestines spilled from his stomach and onto the ground. His lungs and liver were missing, as was his head. One thigh had been devoured by the bear.

"Smell's awful," Marv said. "We've got to call the State Police again."

"Yeah. I have the number."

I punched the number into my cell phone and hit the call button.

The call center answered on the first ring. "State Police, Albany Division."

"This is Bart Jones. You guys responded to a possible bear kill at Mariaville Lake maybe ten days ago. We got another one. Same place. Deceased human. Male. Decapitated and partially eaten by a bear. Request you send a team. Maybe you should send ENCON out here to destroy the bear. He seems to enjoy human flesh."

"What's your name again? Can you give me an address?"

I gave the call center staffer the pertinent information. He said he'd call me right back. He did. "We have three cars on their way. Should be there in fifteen minutes."

Marv escorted Naomi back down the hillside, while I remained behind to protect the body from further damage by the bear.

It took the State Police thirty minutes to arrive. I could hear their car tires on Naomi's gravel driveway and their excited voices as they began to climb the hillside a few minutes later. Shortly, four men appeared, three in state police uniforms and one clearly a forest ranger.

The lead officer stuck out his hand. "Reingard," he said. "Are you Jones?"

"Yeah."

"You touch anything?"

"Yeah, we rolled him over, using a stick. I touched his boots. That's all."

"So, he was basically face down when you found him?"

"More on his side. I think the bear rolled him to protect his next meal."

The ranger approached. "That would be correct. The bear would roll him to keep birds from having access to the feeding site. Leaves would help to hide the body, as well as keep other animals from feeding."

"Jones, this is Simpson, from ENCON," Reingard said. "He's the bear expert."

I said hello and shook Simpson's hand.

"Do I have correct information? Is this the second body this bear has fed on in the past month?"

"Yes," I said.

"I've got the report from the first body in my vehicle," Reingard said. "It was mostly bones that were left. It was decapitated. Head was found up above…on the other side of the highway."

"This one is decapitated, too," I said.

"I'm seeing a pattern here," Reingard said.

He wasn't as astute as I had hoped. "What do you see?"

"Somebody is killing people and throwing them over the guardrail up above. They roll down here and the bear finds them."

"Actually," Simpson said, "the bear drags the bodies here. When bears make a kill, usually a deer or small game, they drag their kill to a safe place where they feed on it for several days. I'd say the bear dragged the body from close to the road up there, and this is his safe feeding place."

"You got anybody looking for the head?" I asked.

"We'll do it after we collect this guy."

One of the other troopers began taking pictures of the body from all angles. Once the pictures were taken, the third trooper searched the body for identification.

"He's clean. No wallet. Only identifying marks are his tattoos. Gotta name or something on his fingers: M-NOZ. Anybody speak Spanish?"

I shook my head. I wanted to tell the troopers what I knew, but I bit my tongue, not wanting to bring the State Police down on French or Scentless Waste Removal. After the events of last night, it would not take too bright a guy to eyeball Scentless as a probable mob operation.

"Wrap him up," Reingard ordered.

"Hold on," Simpson said. He bent down and took measurements of the abdominal cavity. Then he took a couple of pictures of his own, using his cell phone camera. "Okay, you can wrap it now. Looks like a bear in the three hundred fifty pound range. Maybe four years old."

The two troopers put on nitrile gloves and unfolded a nylon body bag. As they struggled to roll the body into the bag without damaging something which would irritate a medical examiner, I heard a noise from our left. Reingard and Simpson must have heard it too because we all looked in unison.

The roar from the bear caught us by surprise. We heard snapping twigs and saw saplings crash to the forest floor and then suddenly he was on us. He hit Reingard squarely in the chest with two paws, throwing him to the ground at least ten feet away. Unarmed, I backed away as quickly as I could. The bear turned toward Simpson and then reared on its hind legs and walked toward him. Simpson struggled for his pistol, which was strapped onto his equipment belt. As he freed it and pulled it out, the bear slapped at his hand, sending the revolver into the brush.

"BANG! BANG!...BANG! Simpson stepped to his right and the bear fell forward onto all fours. BANG! The fourth shot caused it to fall onto its chin. Its body shuddered and it collapsed to the ground. Its huge chest rose and fell twice and then all movement stopped.

Both troopers who had been wrestling with Muñoz's body were holding forty-five caliber semiautomatics in their hands. They quickly approached Reingard. "Are you hurt?" one asked his superior officer.

"Just my pride," Reingard said.

They holstered their pistols and helped Reingard to his feet.

"Oooh. I may have a cracked rib."

The troopers released him and Reingard stood erect, his right shoulder was rolled forward and his left hand was pressing against his right side.

One of the troopers brushed dirt and leaves from Reingard's butt and trousers' legs, as a mother would clean her dirty child.

I turned to look at Simpson, who was retrieving his revolver from the moist leaves on the forest floor. Blood was trickling from his right forearm.

"How are you doing, Simpson?" I asked.

"Got a few scratches. Probably going to need a couple of stiches. I'm glad Brer Bear didn't get a direct hit, or I might have lost an arm."

Reingard called for backup assistance and an ambulance.

The Duanesburg Rescue Squad arrived first, their sirens blaring as they pulled into Naomi's driveway. Marv Faulkner led the three paramedics up the hill to our location.

"What we got here?" the leader of the EMT's asked. He was a tall man with a large gut and a weed patch of sandy brown hair. He wore a standard brown uniform shirt with blue jeans and camouflage hunting boots.

I pointed at Reingard. "Possible broken ribs over there." Then I pointed at Simpson. "But Simpson sustained some pretty nasty gashes from that bear."

The EMT stood for a moment, studying the mound of dark brown fur. "Big fella. Would make a nice mount if I could have him."

"Sorry buddy," Simpson said. "We've got to take him to the State labs for examination. Got to try to figure out what made him a maneater."

The EMT walked over to Simpson. "Show me your arm."

Simpson held it out. The EMT used scissors to cut

Simpson's sleeve off at the elbow.

"Whooee, he got you good." He turned to the other two EMT's. "Johnson, you go check out those ribs on that there fella. Parker, you help me with this here fella. Looks like his arm is gonna need a hundred stitches."

Obviously, Simpson's wounds were more than minor. The two EMT's cleaned them with peroxide, and then field-dressed them until they could get Simpson to a doctor.

When they were done, we all began the trek down the hill to the ambulance.

Reingard refused to be carried down the hill on a stretcher but chose to prove his machismo by walking by himself, though everyone could see he was in pain.

A few minutes later, we reached Naomi's driveway. The back-up squad of troopers arrived at the same time. Simpson was assisted into the ambulance for the trip to the hospital emergency room in Schenectady. After Reingard gave his back-up team instructions, he climbed into the ambulance with Simpson, and the ambulance exited the driveway, hitting its siren about the time its tires found the hard-surface road.

Faulkner and I led the three-man back-up team of troopers up the hill to Muñoz's body.

"That's a darn large animal," Faulkner said as he took pictures of the bear with his cell phone camera. "Think it's safe to build a campfire now?"

I nodded. "Yeah, it's probably safe now. I think your family would enjoy a relaxing fire after all this excitement."

The troopers began the task of stuffing the partially eaten corpse into the body bag. "Where's the head?" one asked aloud.

"We're supposed to look for it on the road up top," another one replied. "We'll drive up there after this mess is in the trunk."

When we were all assembled down below, Naomi Malbrook brought cups of lemonade for anyone who wanted some. And Anna Faulkner offered homemade oatmeal cookies which she and Emma Rose had just pulled from the oven. I've never known a uniformed officer to refuse such hospitality.

The back-up squad called ENCON for assistance with removing the bear's carcass. They arrived an hour later with a front-end loader on a flatbed to make the job easier.

I stayed below while they did their work. But then, as the rangers were coming back down the hill with the dead bear heaped into the bucket, the local press arrived, clued to the events and their location by the police and rescue scanners they monitored.

"Who killed the bear?" one reporter asked the troopers.

"Who'd he eat?" another one asked the ENCON men.

A woman dressed in a navy-blue business suit held a microphone to Marv's mouth while he responded to questions about his role in the event and his feelings about the safety of renting cabins on the lake.

"Been coming here for more than twenty years," he replied. "Never had any problems with wildlife, and I expect we won't have any more this year, not since this bad boy has been taken out of commission."

It was a big day for Mariaville, but not the sort of negative publicity the community sought.

I tried to avoid the cameras by sitting on the front

stoop of the Faulkner's cabin with Emma Rose. She asked about the events of the day, and I tried to explain what the different emergency crews were doing.

"Can I see the bear?" she asked.

We held hands and walked over to the front-end loader. I lifted her to my shoulders so she could look into the bucket, about five feet off the ground.

"Hi, mister bear," she said as she reached out and petted the bear's head and neck. Then she pulled her hand back and wiped it on her shirt. "His hair is coarse and sticky. I thought it would be soft like a teddy bear's."

"I guess he needs a bath," I replied.

She shook her finger at the bear. "Not in my tub. There's not enough room."

Chapter Thirteen

At six in the morning, Caesar French had Otto Horstmann pull a recently acquired Onondaga Trash truck into the painting cubicle at the Scentless warehouse. He ordered two men, Carlos Santa Cruz and Abdul Maalak, to use angle grinders to cut deep crevices into the steel sides of the truck. Sparks flew in beautiful arcs as they did their work, and when they were finished, six hours later, the truck's sides had the appearance of a giant hand grenade. Then Pepe Barbado and Levi Goldman used wallboard trowels to fill the crevices with quick-drying drywall compound and smoothed them with a wet cloth. The compound was baked under hot lights for an hour. Next, French's painter went to work, spraying the entire truck with a new coating of green and yellow paint and carefully crafting the Onondaga Trash Company's logo onto its sides. When he was finished, the truck baked under hot lights and fans for an hour.

At six o'clock in the evening, Otto Horstmann climbed into the cab of the Onondaga Trash truck and pressed a lever which opened the packer panel in the rear of the truck. Two men entered the truck's empty body carrying duffel bags of white C-4 plastic explosives. They did their work quickly and efficiently.

Then at seven thirty, Horstmann and Santa Cruz drove the freshly painted truck out of Willow Falls and took back roads into Albany. On the way, they drove through several new housing developments to send dust onto the freshly painted truck. Finally, they pulled the truck into the parent parking lot of Maria Teresa Catholic School. It was 8:00 p.m. They shut the motor and closed the cab, leaving the keys in the ignition.

Santa Cruz made the sign of the cross and kissed the statue of the Holy Mother which hung on the silver chain around his neck. "I don't like leaving this truck near a church. There's something unholy about it."

"We must follow El Escondido's orders, precisely as he has given them."

Carlos nodded, lit a cigarette, and sat on the truck's running board.

Otto bummed a cigarette. Carlos shook his pack until the filtered end of a cigarette popped up. Otto plucked it out of the pack and then took match from Carlos and lit it with his thumbnail. They stood smoking but not talking for a couple of minutes. The sound of tires on asphalt alerted them to the arrival of a black four-door Jeep Wrangler, which weaved through the parking lot and came to rest fifteen feet from them. When its interior light came on, the men saw two heavily armed men seated in the front. Otto and Carlos climbed into the back seat, and then the Wrangler quietly drove away. There was no commotion and none of the neighbors noticed.

At eight thirty, the Albany police received a call from an anonymous source complaining about a trash truck sitting empty at the Catholic school. "It looks suspicious," the person told them.

The police found the vehicle and then called the Onondaga Trash Company's emergency number.

"Hello? Onondaga Trash. If this is an emergency, please wait and our answering service will assist you."

When the answering service responded, Police Sergeant Maxwell asked for his call to be forwarded immediately to the owner or general manager of Onondaga trash company. The operator hung up.

Two minutes later, the return call came in. "This is Peter Leon, general manager of Onondaga Trash. Is there a problem?"

"This is Sergeant Maxwell, Albany Police. You can't leave one of your trash trucks unattended in the parking lot of a Catholic school. If it's broken down, you need to have it towed away for repair."

"One of our trucks is at a Catholic School? Where? I'm not aware any of our trucks is broken down."

Sargeant Maxwell gave Leon the address. "I'll be waiting here until you arrive with your tow truck."

"I'm sorry for the inconvenience, officer. We'll be there shortly."

Twenty minutes passed and then a large, unmarked wrecker pulled into the lot at Mother Teresa School. It backed up to the front end of the trash truck. Two men climbed out and smiled at Sergeant Maxwell who was leaning against the front quarter panel of his cruiser. The men then began the work of setting straps under the front end of the trash truck.

Before their work was finished, Peter Leon arrived in an Army green first-generation Hummer. He quickly climbed out and greeted Sergeant Maxwell. "Thank you for finding this truck. It was stolen from us this past week. We're glad to have it back."

"Stolen? And you didn't report it?"

"We were confident it would show up, probably in some out of the way place. You know how kids are. Somebody took it for a joy ride and left it here. They're probably filming us right now and will post the truck rescue on YouTube."

One of the Onondaga workers hurried up to Leon, speaking in Spanish.

Pointing at the truck, Leon responded in Spanish and the man hurried back to his fellow worker.

"What did he say to you?" Sergeant Maxwell asked.

"He asked if he had permission to lift the front end and haul the truck back to our warehouse. I gave him permission."

Actually, he had informed Leon they had inspected the underside of the truck and found no explosives. They had also inspected the cab and discovered the keys were in the ignition. Then Leon had ordered him to haul the truck away.

When the tow truck reached Onondaga Trash Company's Albany headquarters, the truck was parked alongside the administrative building, where it sat unattended. Peter Leon would have it fully inspected in the morning.

Chapter Fourteen

Two days after finding the second body on the hill behind Naomi Malbrook's home, I drove to Cabrillo Construction. Caesar French had followed my suggestions. The eight-foot-high chain link fence which surrounded the square block of Cabrillo Construction's property was now sporting rolls of razor wire, stretched like Slinkies from corner to corner. In each corner he had erected temporary guard towers, and in each tower stood two men, looking in opposite directions. It truly looked like a war zone.

I pulled up to the entry gate. A man wearing a flak jacket under a green windbreaker approached my Bronco. "Good morning, Jones. Mr. French said you would be coming. You armed?"

I had a forty-five semiautomatic in my glove compartment. "No," I fibbed. "No weapons on me."

"You should be armed. Danger hides at every corner."

He turned and signaled to two men. They unlocked a chain and rolled the gate open so I could drive through. I pulled up to the main office, where sandbags now filled the windows to protect French's secretary.

I walked in the door. "Hey, Laverne. How are you?"

She was in a white dotted Swiss dress and wearing a flak jacket of conflicting drab green color.

"Nervous as all hell. I didn't sign on for combat duty

when I took this job."

"You're not thinking about quitting, are you?"

"Lord, no. Where could I go to get a receptionist job that pays like I'm a teacher?"

She buzzed French to let him know I was coming into the back area. When she got the go-ahead, she hit a button and the door to the office area buzzed open. It was another new safety feature, intended to buy a few more seconds of time if the front office suddenly were overrun with opposition forces.

French was at his office door when I entered the hallway. He was in military fatigues and resembled the picture on Che Guevara tee shirts worn by college kids.

"Good morning, Jones. Come in. I keep my door locked now."

"I don't blame you."

He sat down, but he oozed an aura of nervous energy. "You got news for me?"

"Yeah. Muñoz is dead."

He leaned back in his chair, his eyes suddenly welling with tears. "I already assumed that. Where's his body?"

"The State Troopers took it. It was at the same place in Mariaville where they found Perez. His ring finger was severed, but you know that. He was also missing his head. The troopers were looking for it this morning. I'm not sure if they found it."

"Mother of God, his killers used the same dumping ground? Would anybody really do that?"

"Yes, the same place. And the same bear ate him for dinner last night. But the bear is now dead."

His eyes opened wide. "Did you shoot it?"

"No, two State Troopers did it. I wasn't armed at the

time."

French gave me a stern look. "You should always be armed these days, my friend."

"Your main gate guard told me the same thing this morning."

He opened his left hand toward me. "You need a pistol? I got a couple you can carry."

"Thanks, but I've got a forty-five. I just need to start carrying it."

"Yeah, you do. You don't look like a cop anymore, but someday some guy you sent up is going to recognize you and try to put a hole between your eyes."

I nodded. "You're probably right. I'll start carrying again today."

French smiled in approval.

"So, besides fortifying your compound, what have you been doing?" I asked.

"I already got a shitload of new Scentless trashcans, special order. They were distributed yesterday, and the regular pick-up schedule has been resumed. I didn't lose a single customer."

"That's remarkable."

"Yes, and as you suggested, my attorney met with the city, and they paid my overtime expenses to clean up all the burned cans and debris from my customers' homes."

I smiled. "So, you actually won the battle."

"Actually, I made money on the deal because I don't pay overtime."

I knew these events were only battles and the war had just begun. "How do you think Onondaga is going to come at you next time?"

"They might not get a chance…"

"What are you up to?"

He folded his arms across his chest. "Nothing I would admit to. It's better if you don't know."

Suddenly I knew French had planned and probably set in motion some type of retaliation for the attacks against his men and his company. I had to agree with him. It was best I didn't know his plans. After all, on paper I was still a police officer, and I did not need to be complicit in something clandestine. I hoped his actions would be something the capital region could tolerate.

"I'm still trying to identify Perez's killer. It would be nice to bring him to justice."

"Don't you mean 'bring him to me?' "

"Yeah, that's what I meant."

"We got word Onondaga is sending Los Cuernos our way again tonight."

"You have informants everywhere, don't you?"

"This was the sister of one of Onondaga's soldiers. She's been sleeping with one of my lieutenants. She told him because she didn't want him to get hurt. Begged him to stay with her and not come to our warehouse tonight."

"You want me here to be another gun in your army?"

"No. This is our war, not yours. You stay home tonight. They may not be able to come tonight, anyway."

****

I was in the kitchen of my camp microwaving a bag of popcorn. I had just finished watching a rerun of Gunsmoke, where Matt Dillon had arrested two men who tried to blow open a safe at the Dodge City Bank. It was almost eleven o'clock, so from the kitchen I used the remote to change channels to the evening news. The lead story was about an explosion at Onondaga Trash in

Albany. I shut down the stove and increased the volume to be sure I didn't miss anything.

When the commentator turned the feed over to the on-the-scene reporter, Myra Yodor, the camera showed the side of the main Onondaga warehouse, which had been blown open. Flames and black smoke were billowing from the opening, reminding me of the Pentagon during 9/11. Firemen from two companies had answered the call. I could see three streams of water arching from the ground into the cavern of flames and another spraying from a ladder extended from the back of a firetruck. Emergency lights were flashing up and down the street in the late evening darkness.

"Six people were killed and eight injured this evening," Myra reported, "when an Onondaga trash truck exploded beside the warehouse where it was waiting its turn to be refilled with diesel for tomorrow's run. Investigators are unsure about the cause of the explosion, but some suspect a fuel leak, while others suspect an incendiary device of some sort had found its way into the truck from someone's trash can."

The picture switched to the Chief of Albany's Fire Station No. Three. His face was covered in sweat and soot. "We were able to pull several potential victims from the building before they died of smoke inhalation. We're unsure what kind of accelerant was inside the building at the time of the explosion, but whatever it was, it has caused major destruction to the building's infrastructure, probably rendering it unsafe for future utilization."

The picture returned to Myra Yodor. "Dan, the police tell me they will be investigating this explosive fire from several angles, including the possibility of arson because Onondaga's customer base has dropped by more than thirty percent since the arrival of its major competitor, Scentless Waste Removal, only a few months ago."

When the news segued into a story about the closure of another Catholic school, I shut the television.

"Jesus H. Christ, what have you done, Caesar?" I said aloud. "You lost three and eliminated six of the opposition. Is that how it works: two for one?"

Without doubt, Onondaga would retaliate. If they followed the same two-for-one philosophy, the next event would be a massacre.

Chapter Fifteen

Helen called me at nine o'clock in the morning. I didn't answer because I was outside skipping stones into the lake and didn't hear my phone ring. She left a message.

"Hey, Jonesy. It's you-know-who. How come you don't call me anymore? Got some news for you. Also need to talk with you about those headless horsemen who were found out your way. Give me a call when you've got some free time."

When I came inside, I poured myself a cup of coffee and returned her call.

"Oh, so you aren't dead," she said without first saying "Hello."

"No, I'm not dead. How are things at work? I haven't heard anything from the chief. Nothing. I guess he doesn't love me."

"That's part of why I'm calling. Chief wants you to call his secretary and set up an appointment to come in. He wants to see you before the end of the week."

"Why is he suddenly so anxious to see me? He's been dragging this rip out much longer than he should have, and of course, the union could give a flying you-know-what about me. So, they haven't been pushing him to bring me back."

"Just call Louise and set up the appointment."

"Roger. Will do."

"Got a problem I want to talk with you about, too, but not over the phones. Want to meet at Ruby's?"

"Yeah. Right now a hotdog would taste mighty good. Twelve o'clock?"

"Sounds good, Jonesy. See you then."

After Helen hung up, I called the chief's secretary, Louise, and set up an appointment to meet with him at nine in the morning on Thursday. Then I called my union representative, Fat Georgie Hughes, and told him when to meet me at the chief's office. Although he said he would be there, his tone sounded somewhat non-committal.

At eleven thirty I drove into Willow Falls and parked at Ruby's Red Hots. Helen was already there, so I walked inside and saw her sitting at our usual stools near the end of the counter. She was wearing a black spandex jumpsuit that fit her like it had been painted on. But her feet were stuffed into black and gold leopard print tennis shoes. I pointed at them as I sat down.

"Where'd you get those babies?" I asked.

"You don't like them? Got them on the internet. They came from Pakistan. Cost me twelve dollars and came with free shipping."

"I've never seen anything quite like them. They look comfortable."

"Looks can be deceiving."

"Tell me about it."

The waitress appeared and took our orders. Instead of my usual hotdog, I opted for a burger with meat sauce and onions.

"Would that be a plain burger or an all-meat burger?"

I didn't know burgers could come with oatmeal or

something else as a filler. "All meat."

"How about you, honey?" she asked Helen. "You want the usual two hotdogs with meat sauce and mustard, hold the onions?"

"That would be fine," Helen replied. "And a diet cola."

"Sure."

The waitress looked at me.

"I'll do water with ice."

She turned toward the chef and shouted, "Two wieners with mustard and sauce, and a cow pie all the way."

By the time she walked fifteen feet from our seats at the counter to the chef's station, our orders were waiting for her to pick up. She quickly snatched them and returned, sliding them in front of us like she had done it a million times before. "Either of you want hot sauce?"

"Please," I replied.

She reached in front of a guy two seats down from us and plucked a small bottle of hot sauce from the counter in front of him. She set it down in front of me, leaning over so I could get an eyeful of her cleavage. "There you go, handsome. You can have anything you want."

"Ask her if she's had a penicillin shot lately," Helen whispered.

I smiled, sprinkled a few drops of hot sauce on the meat, and then took a bite of my burger. The meat was thin and melted in my mouth as though it contained no meat at all. I wondered if the chef had slipped in a non-meat burger and charged me the extra fifty cents for an all-meat one. But this just was not the sort of place you would ask that kind of question.

Helen wiped some grease from her lips and then got down to business. "You know those two bodies which were found up your way?"

"Perez and Muñoz?"

"Yeah. They both worked for Cabrillo Construction. One was reported missing. The other one went missing, but Cabrillo didn't report it. Then, last week just about every Cabrillo trash can in Schenectady was burned to a puddle of melted plastic. What kind of mess are they into, Jonesy?"

I swallowed a bite of my burger. "Why are you asking me? You work for Willow Falls, anyway. Sounds like Schenectady's problem to me."

"Well, for one, the new ride of yours is registered to Cabrillo Construction. Are you working for them?"

Helen and I had established one rule during our working relationship—we did not lie to each other. Well, not entirely.

So, I told her the truth. Well, not entirely. "Caesar French loaned me the Bronco when the department recalled my sedan. A guy in my financial situation can't be too choosy."

Helen wiped some grease from her lips. "So, now do you owe him? And when do you expect him to collect on his goodwill? He knows you're a cop, and eventually he'll expect you to do something that's probably against department policies."

"I don't know for certain, but I think he already has a mole in the Department."

"What makes you say that?"

"You know the day the chief put me on long-term rip?"

Helen nodded.

"French called me while I was driving home from the meeting with Chief Comstock. He already knew I was on semi-permanent furlough, and he called to offer me a job."

"No kidding?"

"No kidding."

Helen took another bite of her hotdog and chased it with a swallow of cola. "So, what do you do for him? You're not into anything illegal, are you?"

"No, he hasn't asked me to do anything illegal. So far, I've been helping him identify what's happened to missing company property, and I'm investigating the deaths and dismemberments of those two guys you mentioned."

Helen looked concerned. "That's police work."

"I'm sure the State Police are trying to solve the murders of those two men who were found in their jurisdiction, but there's no law against a company's hiring a private detective to ferret out information the police can't obtain without warrants and without following their ethical guidelines. A detective doesn't have to work within those parameters."

"When the chief finds out what you're doing, he's going to crucify you."

"Yeah, and if I weren't doing this, I'd be collecting aluminum cans from the roadside to try to eat. You got any better ideas?"

"Oh, Jonesy, this isn't good."

****

After lunch I drove to Cabrillo Construction. As I turned onto Sledge Street, I saw an orange four-door late model Chevy pickup truck, loaded with at least four men. I thought I saw the barrel of a rifle or shotgun leaning against the glass of the rear window. I slowed as I passed and recognized the shaved head and rectangular jaw of the driver. He was the guy who had used a bat to break the rear window of my Bronco when I visited the Onondaga Trash Company a few weeks ago. The presence of the truck and its men was not a good sign.

I was not sure if the men in the truck spotted me. But just in case, I turned into the entrance of Cabrillo Construction and told the guards about the truck which was scoping out the place. A minute later, two Jeep Commandos left Cabrillo's front gate to send the occupants of the truck back to Albany. They must have gotten the message because the moment the Jeeps left the gate, the orange pickup pulled away from the curb and hightailed it out of the neighborhood.

I parked my Bronco and then walked through the main office. I waved quickly at Laverne before I walked through the door to the back area. She nodded and waved at me. I knocked twice on French's door, but he did not answer, so I continued into the warehouse area.

French was talking with two of his men, both armed with AK-47s. I paused until he was finished and then walked up to him. He was dressed in green denims and a green jungle shirt, covered with an army surplus flak jacket.

"Good afternoon, Caesar," I said.

He turned to me. He looked fatigued. "You got news for me?"

"Yeah. Both the State Police and the Willow Falls police are now investigating the deaths of Perez and Muñoz. Willow Falls seems to have connected the burning of your trashcans in Schenectady to the murders. I'm willing to bet they'll try to connect the explosion at

Onondaga Disposal to the burning of your trashcans. I imagine they'll be dropping in on you any day now. I'm sure they'll have a barrage of questions for you."

"Those poor bastards at Onondaga," he replied solemnly. "I called to offer them some assistance, but their phones don't work. Thought maybe we could work their trash routes until they're back up and running."

"Would you like me to find the personal phone number of their owner?"

"No need to do that. I've already sent him a letter of condolences and offered help."

"A truckload of his men were scoping out your compound when I came in. Your guys scared them away."

"*Our* guys, Jones. You're one of us now."

"Yeah, okay…*our* guys scared them away."

"Good. We don't need more trouble at the moment."

I looked around his warehouse. All the first-floor windows were boarded and all doors were locked. "When I drove into the compound, the outside looked like a war zone. You seem prepared for just about anything they could throw at you."

"Maybe. If they come by air or through the sewers, we could be vulnerable."

I put my finger to my lips. "Shhh. They could be listening as we speak."

"You really think so?"

"If they have a bug in here, or if they've stationed some guys on a rooftop nearby with a dish, there's no telling what they could hear."

"See, Jones, you *do* think of everything. Maybe I got to set up a listening station near their headquarters to find out what they're planning."

"Not a bad idea. Wish I had thought of it."
Caesar smiled.

Chapter Sixteen

I headed back to Mariaville and stopped at Naomi Malbrook's cabin. She was up to her hips in the water, pulling weeds and plopping them on her dock. Little Emma Rose Faulkner was helping her by dragging the weeds on a tarp to the burn pit behind Naomi's cabin.

"Hey, Naomi, would you like a hand?" I shouted.

"Sure, if you want to give me half an hour. I've already been out here for ninety minutes, and I'm close to calling it a day."

I took my wallet and phone out of my pants pockets, removed my shirt, shoes, and socks, and rolled my cotton twill trousers' legs up to my knees. I walked into the cool water. The mud squished up between my toes, and I felt like a kid again.

"Water's nice," I said as I approached Naomi and Emma.

Emma straightened the tarp on the dock. "Hi, Mr. Jones. Catch any bad guys?"

"Hi, Emma. Not today. Seen any more bears?"

"Think there was just the one," Naomi said. "Emma's parents have had a campfire every night since the nuisance bear was hauled away. Isn't that right Emma?"

"We've had s'mores every night."

"I haven't had a s'more since I was a kid," I said.

"They're good, that's for sure, but if you have them

every night they're not as special as they once were."

The kid sounded like a philosopher.

"Have you had any more visits from the State Troopers or the ENCON police?" I asked.

"Things here have gotten back to normal," Naomi replied. "Nothing to do except pull and burn weeds every day." She reached deep into the water with both hands and brought up a tangle of lake grass and milfoil. "See the red stems on this milfoil? That's Eurasian Milfoil. It's the invasive stuff. Some of the milfoil has green or white stems. That's domestic milfoil. It's not as invasive, but I still pull it out. I hate weeds."

I reached down into the water and grabbed two handfuls of weeds. When I brought them to the surface, the water around my legs became muddy. I tossed the tangled wad of green onto the tarp. "Have you ever thought about composting the milfoil instead of burning it? Then maybe you could use it for fertilizer."

She pulled another clump of milfoil from the water and plopped it on Emma's tarp. "I hate this stuff so much I don't see any good in it. By burning it, I send it right to…well, you know where."

I laughed. "Yeah, I guess I do."

"Yeah, you send it right to 'h-e-l-l-o'," Emma said.

Naomi and I looked at each other and chuckled. We both had just been reminded that kids have big ears.

****

I pulled weeds with Naomi and Emma until Mrs. Faulkner called Emma in for dinner. Naomi and I then walked out of the water, and I promised her I would be back again in a few days to continue helping with her daily chore.

I drove home to my cabin, collected my clothes and

shoes, and walked inside. In my bedroom, I changed into dry clothes and then hung my twill trousers to dry on the deck railing out back. Then I popped a beer and turned on the six-o'clock news. Nothing much was happening locally—just a couple of murders of women by their boyfriends in small communities. It was becoming so commonplace society was becoming numb to it. Well, I certainly was, anyway.

When the national news came on, I popped a second beer and listened to more mind-numbing reporting. The congressional vote on abortion was finally over and members of the winning side were accusing members of the losing side of absurdities and calling for their heads, either through impeachment or social disenfranchisement. The world I had known as a kid was completely gone, and I couldn't see any sense in continuing to listen to the stuff being doled out on national television. I longed for college and professional football to return, but it was a couple of months away.

I heard tires squealing outside on the pavement, probably one hundred yards away. Soon the sound of tires, now on gravel, grew louder. Suddenly the air was riveted by the Pop! Pop! Pop! Pop! Pop! of semiautomatic gun fire. My kitchen windows shattered. Shards of glass and pieces of wood and insulation flew above me. I rolled off my sofa and onto the floor. The sliding glass doors to my deck took several rounds and then collapsed to the floor. One large pane fell outside and another inside. My television screen went black, two holes in its center. I heard tires kicking stones against something metallic. The shooting had stopped. I ran to the kitchen window and looked toward the main road. An orange four-door pickup truck turned toward the city, burning rubber on the asphalt.

I called the State Police and reported the incident, suggesting they send cars to watch the highway into Albany for a four-door orange Chevy pickup with men carrying automatic weapons. They said they would send a trooper out to make a report. He arrived an hour later.

Trooper Nathan Walker arrived with no fanfare—no sirens, no cherries flashing—and he was in no particular hurry. He knocked on the front door. I peered out through a bullet hole and saw he was in uniform. I opened the door. "Come in. There's lots of fresh air inside my cabin tonight."

Trooper Walker stuck a probe into a bullet hole in my door. Then he probed one in the kitchen wall. "Looks like three-oh-eight caliber," he said. "Probably an old AR-15 or an M16." He jotted something in his notepad. "Maybe both."

He walked through the living area and into my bedroom, where the window was shattered, and the wall was punctured by at least a dozen bullet holes. He bent down with his pocketknife and pried a bullet out of my bed's headboard. "They hoped to take you out."

I nodded. "Did you guys get the pickup truck?"

"Nope. The description didn't come in until half an hour after the incident. They were long gone by then."

"It shouldn't be too hard to find an orange four-door Chevy pickup in the capital region."

"I'll tell headquarters you said that. Meanwhile, I'm trying to count bullet holes and assess damages for my report. You'll need it for the insurance company, anyway. Any more bullets in the furniture?"

I shrugged and let him do his work. When he finished writing his report, he handed me a carbon copy.

"Your insurance agent will need this."

I had just recently purchased renter's insurance. The ink on my application was barely dry and already I would be submitting a claim. I was certain the company would cancel my insurance immediately.

"Thanks."

"Any idea who did this?" Trooper Walker asked. "I mean, how many were there? How long did the incident last? Who would want to see you dead?"

I was pretty sure it was the guys from Onondaga Disposal, but I couldn't blame them, or I would be opening a bigger can of worms for French. "Officially I'm a detective with the Willow Falls PD. Just about anybody I ever collared could want me dead. I didn't see anybody because I was too busy dodging bullets. When the shooting stopped, I saw the orange pickup leaving the area like the driver was being chased by the police."

"Maybe he thought he would be."

I smiled. "Maybe."

Then I remembered my Bronco. "Did they damage my truck?"

I hurried outside. Walker followed me with his flashlight. We slowly circled my Bronco. It appeared to be unscathed. I thought they would have taken out their anger on my ride, as well, but they hadn't. Maybe they respected a high-quality restoration. Maybe they just didn't think about it. If the shoe had been on the other foot, I would have at least taken out the tires so the guy I was trying to hit could not chase me if I had been unsuccessful in killing him. I suppose I should have chased after them, but they would have been shooting semiautomatic weapons at me as I gained on them. No doubt I would have ended up in the morgue.

Chapter Seventeen

On Thursday at nine, I met Fat Georgie Hughes at Chief Comstock's office. Comstock's secretary, Louise, asked us to sit in a couple of hard-back chairs and wait until he was ready for us. The head of personnel came into the area, too, but she was sent right in. I assumed she and Comstock had to powwow before they brought me in.

When he was ready for me, he buzzed Louise. She picked up her receiver and nodded. "You may go in now, gentlemen."

I walked in ahead of Georgie. I hoped he would see it as a sign of disrespect.

The chief was sitting behind his desk. The personnel lady was to his left. I sat in a chair in front of the desk. Georgie sat beside me.

"You've had a long cooling off period," Comstock said. "Your next employer is going to appreciate your calmer attitude and demeanor."

"You mean you're firing me?"

"No. The city has been petitioned by the Anti-fascists and Black Lives Matter, and the city council has caved by agreeing to defund our police force by twenty percent. You're not being fired. Your position has been terminated by the Defund the Police movement."

"But Chief…"

"I was ready to bring you back a couple of weeks

ago, Jones, but this reduction in our budget has forced me to let fifteen of my finest officers go."

"What about Helen Martin? Has she been defunded, too?"

"No. She was next to last on the list, but we've accepted two late notifications of retirement, and one of them saved her butt."

"So, do I lose my retirement?"

The head of personnel cleared her throat. "As much as it pains me to say this, Detective Jones, you were fully vested last week…Friday, I believe…so your retirement benefit stands. When you reach the age of fifty-five, you can petition to collect retirement benefits to the tune of twenty percent of your current fulltime salary."

It wasn't much, but I figured if I make it to fifty-five, a little extra beer money would come in handy.

"Is there any other good news?"

"Yes," Comstock replied, "we've negotiated with the health plan provider, and you will receive full health benefits through the end of this calendar year. That's worth six or seven thousand dollars to you."

"Well, that's something."

"And the city council has agreed to severance pay matching the amount of vacation time you have saved up, which in your case…" Comstock looked at a sheet of paper. "Well, it looks like you don't have any vacation time saved up, Jones. Sorry about that."

I wanted to jump across the desk and strangle him. "Is there any chance of recall?"

"There is always the possibility the city council will change its mind and rescind the Defund the Police order. If it does, we'll rehire individuals on a first-out, first-rehired basis."

"So where do I stand on the list?"

"You're fourteenth," the personnel lady said.

"So, thirteen get to be rehired before you reach me?"

"Yeah, I'm afraid it looks that way," Comstock said.

I turned to my union representative. "Georgie, you've been sort of quiet through all this. Do you have anything to say? Isn't the union protesting this action? Aren't you suing the city council or something?"

Fat Georgie just shrugged. "I'm one below Martin on the list. The two retirements saved my butt, too."

****

I went to my desk and emptied out my possessions. Actually, I took nothing with me. I simply emptied my drawers into the circular file. Then I stopped by Helen's desk. She wasn't there, so I wrote her a quick farewell note, sealed it in a department envelope, and left it on her chair.

On my way back to Mariaville, I stopped by Cabrillo Construction to see Caesar French. Laverne buzzed me in, and he greeted me when I came through the door.

"I'm glad you're here, Jones. I'm hoping you can help me." He was dressed in a business suit today, black with baby blue pin stripes. No flak jacket.

"Sure. I've got to be at my cabin at two o'clock, but I'll help you in any way I can."

"Remember how you told me the sob story about Vasquez and Morales?"

"You mean the two guys who have the women in their lives hooking to raise money to bring other family members to the States?"

"Yes, Juan Vasquez and Manuel Morales."

I nodded.

"I did as you suggested and sent two of their cousins

the money they needed to fly from Mexico to Canada."

"Why Canada and not New York, maybe Syracuse or Newburgh?"

"It's a long story. The problem is they're in Canada at a motel across the border from a reservation."

"A Native American reservation? What reservation?"

French shuffled through some papers on his desk. "It's the St. Regis Reservation. They're in a motel across the river from St. Regis and I need to get them across the river and down to Willow Falls." He shuffled some more paper and found a post-a-note. "They're in the Elizabeth Regina Motel, room fourteen."

"So, you're asking me to go get them?"

He grinned. "Yes. Tomorrow, if possible."

"Sure, but how do I get them across the border? Do they have visas or passports?"

"No. That's the problem. But if they come through the reservation, they don't need anything. They just need a ride here."

I could see my name in the newspaper, now: *Bart Jones, human trafficker*. "Am I going to have any problems with the reservation police?"

"I don't think so. All you need to do is drive onto the reservation, park at a marina, rent a boat, and cross the river. When you get to the other side, you catch a taxi to the motel, pick them up, and bring them back across the river in the boat. From there, you get back in your car and drive them to Willow Falls. It should be a piece of cake."

"Where do I take them when I get back?"

"Why, here, of course. We will reunite them with their cousins, and they will go live with them while they seek asylum."

I could envision problems arising with this simple piece-of-cake plan, but I wasn't sure what they would be. Hopefully, French had given me enough pertinent information to get the job done. Meanwhile, I was no longer an officially employed police officer, so I couldn't use police status to worm my way out of a pickle with the law if one arose.

"How did you know I needed you today?" French asked.

"I didn't. I had trouble at my place last night and I thought you should know about it."

He waited for me to explain.

"While I was watching the six thirty news last night, an orange Chevy four-door truck parked in front of my cabin and punched at least seventy-four holes in the windows and walls with semiautomatic weapons. I'm going to meet with the insurance adjuster this afternoon. I'm only renting the place and I haven't told the owner about the damages."

"Was it the same orange pickup that was parked down the road?"

"I can't be sure, but it's the only conclusion I can draw."

"Are you asking me for protection?"

"No. I'm letting you know Onondaga Trash has associated me with Scentless Waste Removal, and they tried to take me out. They failed. Meanwhile I have to deal with the cost of repairs to a cabin I don't own."

"But you have insurance?"

"Yeah. I'm hoping they'll cover the renovations."

"Let me know how much they give you, and I'll see if I can get the repairs done for less. Maybe you could make some money on the deal."

"Thanks, Caesar."

"Sure. What are friends for?" He picked up a small notepad and jotted down two names: Rosalba Morales and Juanita Vasquez. "You can get the phone number for the Elizabeth Regina when you get to Canada. The people speak English there."

Chapter Eighteen

The insurance adjuster was waiting for me when I arrived home. He had already inspected the bullet holes on the outside of the house and was jotting notes when I pulled to a stop beside his green Toyota Landcruiser.

"Did you get both sides?" I asked.

"Haven't been around to the lake side yet. Some of the bullets go through?"

"Yeah. Most of them." I stuck out my hand. "Bartholomew Jones, formerly of the Willow Falls Police Department."

"Hi, Mr. Jones. My name is Brewster Smith. You got homeowners or renters insurance?"

"Renters. Does it make a difference?"

"Only in the deductible. Homeowners can pay more for a lower deductible. Renters are stuck with a single rate. Your place is the reason why. Renters just don't take care of a place the way a homeowner does."

"Well, I can assure you I didn't do any of the damages you're listing."

"Maybe not, but your lifestyle was probably partially to blame. It's the same with most renters. Look at your place: It's going to need close to a total rehab, both exterior and interior, I imagine." He looked down at his ballpoint pen. "I reckon I should see the other side. I expect the holes will be bigger."

"Not if they used full metal jackets."

"I suppose you're right about that."

We walked around to the right side of the house. Several bullets had found their way through the siding, cutting six-inch long gullies in the wood before exiting. Mr. Smith jotted more notes. Then we walked around to the lakeside.

"Whoa, look at how they destroyed your sliding glass door. Anybody come in and steal anything while you were gone?"

I had not thought of that possibility. Not many people drive down the road to this cluster of cabins, at least in the winter, but now it was early spring, and traffic would be increasing as people came to their cabins to fix structural problems brought on by winter's cold. There was not much of value to steal in my cabin, anyway. Well, maybe if I were a kid, I would have checked the refrigerator for beer and the cabinets for smokes and liquor.

When Mr. Smith finished taking notes about the outside, we stepped over the broken glass that used to be sliding doors and entered my living area.

"Your interior walls need rehab," he said. "Your television is a mess. So's your sofa. Your refrigerator has bullet holes, and so does your stove. And every window is blown out." He looked up. "At least they spared the ceiling, so the roof is probably okay."

Next, we walked into my bedroom. "Your bed needs replacing. I imagine the mattress is shot up. The dresser needs a new mirror." He looked in the small closet. "Damn, this has been shot up, too." He looked at me and grinned. "Who'd you piss off? You been fooling with some guy's wife or daughter?"

"In my line of work, I arrest a lot of people. I guess

one or two of them found out where I live and sent me a message."

"I'd say so. Let's go check your bathroom."

The bathroom window was gone, the medicine cabinet mirror had been shattered, and the steel shower stall was riddled with holes.

"Total bathroom rehab," he said, shaking his head.

When he was finished, we went outside. Smith began tabulating and writing notes on his tablet.

"How much do you estimate the repairs will cost?" I asked.

"Nearly as much as the cabin cost brand new. And the company isn't going to like this."

"You tell them I'm a cop and a detective, and somebody tried to kill me. That ought to set them straight. I wouldn't do this to my own place."

"Not unless you figured you could get the insurance company to build you a new place, and you did all this damage yourself."

I went to my Bronco, pulled out the police report, and brought it to him. "This is a State Police report about the incident. Be sure you send this to the company as well. It verifies my claim. I expect the company to meet its obligation and repair the damages to this cabin."

"I'll write it up and submit everything this evening. Tomorrow morning I'll bring your police report back. Okay if I just stuff it into your mailbox?"

"Yeah. I won't be here, anyway."

When the adjuster left, I drove to Schenectady, where I bought two pieces of plywood and a large roll of plastic wrap at a discount building supply place. I nailed the plywood to the doorframe of my sliding glass door. Then I stapled plastic wrap across all the broken windows and swept up a trashcan full of broken glass. At midnight there were still small pieces of glass sparkling in the area rugs and under the dinette table, but I was exhausted. I flipped my mattress over so I would not sleep on broken slivers of glass and then I curled up under the sleeping bag I had stored on my closet's top shelf. I hated to leave my place in such a state of disrepair, but I had promised French I would drive to the St. Regis Reservation in the morning. Further clean-up was going to have to wait until I returned.

Chapter Nineteen

There was no direct way to get to the St. Regis Reservation from Mariaville. Like most Native American reservations, it was stuck in the middle of nowhere, so the indigenous had to be creative in how they attracted commerce to their neighborhoods. Usually they offered cheap gas, fireworks, tax-free cigarettes and liquor, and casinos. It seemed to work, at least for the few tribe members who managed to become wealthy by managing those operations.

I left Mariaville at seven in the morning, drove to Amsterdam, and then followed Routes Thirty and Sixty-seven to Saratoga Springs. From there, I took the Northway to Plattsburgh, where I stopped to empty my tanks, buy a cup of coffee, and fill my Bronco with gas. From Plattsburgh, I cut across the top of New York State, letting my cell phone's GPS guide my path. When I reached the St. Regis Mohawk Reservation, it was eleven thirty in the morning.

I pulled into the reservation, expecting some sort of guarded gate. That was not the case. I just drove past a couple of flags flying weakly in the mid-day breeze. The first gas station I came to was "Big Boy's Akwesasne," where gas was advertised at seventy cents per gallon less than I had paid in Plattsburgh. Although I still had half a tank of gas, I pulled in and filled up. It was self-serve. As I waited for my tank to fill, I wondered if the meters were reading the gallons correctly, or if I was paying the full gallon price and receiving only three-quarters of a gallon. I would never know, but the thought of getting untaxed gas was exciting by itself. When the valve shut off, I put the handle back into the machine and then drove to the side of the building and parked.

Inside, Big Boy's was a paleface paradise. Rows of metal shelves offered every variety of illegal fireworks at bargain prices. Floor to ceiling coolers held a wide assortment of beer and wine, again at prices lower than could be found in town. Racks of cigarettes filled the wall behind the cash register. And glass containers were filled with vaping supplies and glass bongs of every description. And everything was untaxed.

I grabbed a twelve-pack of Unibroue Trois Pistoles beer, a dark beer claiming nine percent alcohol content, and went to the register. The cashier was a young woman with chest length coal black hair. Her cheekbones were high and pronounced and her dark brown eyes were bright and crystal clear. I put thirty dollars on the counter. She rang up my purchase and handed me change.

"Thanks," I said. "Would you happen to know if it's possible to charter a fishing boat around here?"

"Sure. Just follow this road to the river, turn left and you'll see a marina with docks and boats. Somebody in there can help you."

I thanked her again, got back into my Bronco, and followed her directions. If I had waited to buy gas and beer, further down the road the price of gas was a nickel less, and I imagined beer was cheaper, too. It was a quick reminder gas is cheaper the further you drive away from the highway.

When I could see the river, I passed by a sign which said, "Welcome to Canada." I could not believe it. The reservation had been plopped directly on the US/Canadian border and existed simultaneously in both countries. And there was no border checkpoint.

At the river, I took a left turn and followed it for a mile before I came to Mohawk Marina. A dozen speedboats were moored to their berths on wooden docks which lined the shore. The water was dark with small ripples whipped up by the wind on the river's surface.

I parked and walked into the white cinderblock building. Inside, metal shelving displayed all sorts of nautical paraphernalia, from life preservers to fishing gear. At the far end, a parts department offered items for boat repair and maintenance. I walked through the door to the docks and saw several men working on their boats.

I didn't want to draw the attention of reservation police or border patrol, so a speedboat was probably not the vessel to try to rent. Instead, I approached a man on a twenty-four-foot pontoon boat. He was dressed in blue jeans and a red tee shirt which sported the Kansas City Chiefs' logo. His belt buckle was a silver oval impregnated with turquoise, like Navajo jewelry. His feet were stuffed into blue Reeboks, no socks.

"Good afternoon," I said.

He lifted his Mets baseball cap. "Hi."

"Do you know where I could rent one of these pontoon boats for the afternoon?"

"These are all private boats. You'll have to go outside of the reservation to find a boat rental place."

"Do you know if anyone here charters their boats?"

"What do you want? A tour of the river?"

"No, I want to go across the river to pick up a friend

who needs a ride to Utica."

"Why don't you just drive over?"

I decided to be truthful. "She doesn't have any papers."

The man dropped the coil of rope he was holding. "Isn't that refreshing."

"Isn't what...?"

"An honest white man."

"Well, does that make me eligible for a ride across the river and back?"

"Maybe. How much you going to pay to smuggle some woman into the USA?"

"How much would a captain charge to take a couple of passengers out fishing in the afternoon?"

"That depends. Is there a lot of luggage? Is she carrying contraband? Is she a hooker?"

"She's the cousin of the man I work for. She's planning to seek asylum in the USA."

"She'd be better off seeking asylum on the reservation. Where is she now?"

"Some motel." I pulled a piece of paper from my pocket and read from it. "The Elizabeth Regina."

"She's in Cornwall, across the river. It's on the other side of Cornwall Island, probably a forty-minute trip by water."

"Would you take me there?"

"Can you promise me no trouble with the law?"

"Nobody can promise you that."

"You still speak the truth. I'll do it for two hundred dollars."

"It's a deal."

"That's per person. And a tank of gas when we get back here."

"Do you count as one of the people?"

He smiled. "No, I'm not going to scalp you."

I laughed and checked my wallet. The guy was expecting me to bring back one woman, but I was bringing back two, so I needed six hundred dollars. I had six hundred fifty, so I was good to go. I would buy his gas with a credit card.

He lifted a blue vinyl bench seat and pulled out two fishing rods. "Put these in the cups, would you?"

I took the two rods and looked at the railing on the boat's stern, where I saw four cups intended for holding rods while trolling. I put one rod on each side of the Evinrude ninety horsepower motor.

"Show me the money," he said.

I opened my wallet and showed him four one-hundred-dollar bills.

The man smiled, cast us off, and accelerated to what seemed like fifty miles per hour.

"My name is Bart," I shouted to him over the motor's whine.

"No names. It's better that way. Call me 'Tonto' and I'll call you 'Kemosabe.' "

This guy was funny. If we lived closer, we might even have become friends. But for the moment, we were just two guys in a business arrangement.

The air on the water was cool, almost cold, and as we rocketed toward the island in front of us, the water became rougher, vibrating my seat quickly and pounding my back with an occasional "oomph" when we hit a large wake from a passing freighter.

Tonto told me we would cut to the right around Cornwall Island and then pass through a channel before crossing the St. Lawrence Seaway.

I should have emptied my tanks before we launched, but I had not thought to do it at the time, and the vibrations made me wish I had.

"Hey, Tonto, can I take a leak?"

He dropped the speed to a crawl, and I opened the boat's side door and did my thing. As I was zipping my fly, he hit the accelerator again and we were back to the races. I nearly fell out the door but managed to catch myself on the side railing. I closed the door and I sat back down on the vinyl seat which hugged the side of the boat.

Once we passed through the channel on the right end of Cornwall Island, the Seaway opened. I could see heavily laden freighters coming and going in both directions. It was a freeway on water, and the conflicting wakes made the going much rougher for our little pontoon boat.

But Tonto seemed to know what he was doing. He aimed us straight at the side of an inbound freighter and then ran along beside it, passing it as though we were in a race. Its rusty steel side loomed above us like a sheer mountain cliff, cutting off the sunlight and driving cold into my bones. Tonto charged onward, finally passing the ship's bow and re-emerging into the warmth of the sun's rays. When we were a hundred yards beyond the bow, Tonto suddenly cut to the right in front of the freighter. Its captain blew its horn. The sound was deafening.

"Ha, ha, ha," Tonto shouted. "They never like it when I do that, but I don't want to jump the wakes they leave behind them."

I smiled and nodded. I was glad I had emptied my tanks because if I hadn't, I would have had wet pants at that moment.

We continued in a westerly direction for ten minutes, and then slowed as we pulled into a shallow inlet with a small marina on the bluff above. Four speedboats were moored to its floating docks.

"Welcome to 'Smugglers Hollow,' " Tonto said. "This is as close as I'm getting to Cornwall. You'll have to go inside to call a cab. I'll wait here until you get back."

While he moored his pontoon boat, I went inside the marina's small shop. The air smelled of beer and bacon. And cigarette smoke. Two men were drinking coffee at a square Formica table.

The proprietor was a short man with a bald head. Dressed in a dark blue tee shirt and a black leather sleeveless vest, he nodded at me as I walked in.

"I heard you pull in. How can I help you?"

I put both palms on his counter. "I need a cab to Cornwall. It'll be a roundtrip fare."

"Three dollars American for the call."

I handed him a five-dollar bill and he gave me two Canadian nickel dollars in return.

"Here's two 'loonies' for you," he said.

I knew I had been taken. Maybe I would buy a beer with them for the return trip across the Seaway.

The cab arrived fifteen minutes later. It was a black Toyota Corolla with a TAXI sign strapped on its roof. The driver opened the passenger side front window. "Are you the gentleman who requested the taxi?"

"That would be me." I opened the door to the back seat and hopped in. "Please take me to the Elizabeth Regina Motel in Cornwall. We are going to pick up a couple of ladies and bring them back here to the marina."

The driver turned out of the parking area and headed

west toward Cornwall. He looked at me in his rearview mirror. "How many ladies are we picking up?"

"Just two."

"Are you related to them or are they hookers?"

"They're related to my boss."

"I wouldn't have booked them into that place, myself. It's used by local hookers. They rent rooms by the hour."

"My boss isn't going to be happy to hear that. If those women have been harmed in any way, there will be hell to pay."

"Just asking, mister. I didn't mean to offend if I did."

"No offense taken. At least you've lowered my expectations of the motel."

We drove for ten minutes and then he turned into a section of Cornwall where no buildings were taller than two stories. The streets were lined with mom-and-pop stores offering meats, vegetables, fruits, baked goods, toys, and hardware. A bookstore stood next to a dry goods store, followed by a bicycle shop and then a liquor store which stood next to a Chinese restaurant. Next, we passed a string of empty storefronts, some with graffiti spray-painted onto the windows or doors. I realized the entire world was suffering from that blight.

At the end of three blocks, the driver turned into the parking lot of the Elizabeth Regina Mo_el. Its neon "t" was not working. I would not call the motel run-down, but it had seen better days and probably had not been renovated since the nineteen sixties. Its main office was located closest to the parking lot entrance, where an overhang protected visitors from snow, rain, or hot sun. However, unlike most motels, which are simply a string of attached rooms with parking spaces outside, the

Elizabeth Regina offered a dozen individual cottages for its guests. Each was constructed of log cabin siding, with a red brick fascia which rose three feet from the ground to the logs. Each roof was steeply pitched, as might be seen in the Swiss Alps. How the motel got its name was a mystery. I thought the Motel Heidi seemed more appropriate.

The taxi driver stopped under the veranda and let me out, promising to wait for me to collect my passengers. I had not paid him yet, so I was certain he would still be there when I came out of the office.

I entered the office. Sitting on the counter was an old-fashioned hand bell with a note that said, "Ring for Service." I hit it twice with my palm.

"Hold your knickers," a woman shouted from the back room.

I saw her shadow first, lumbering on the floor like a waddling duck. Then her feet appeared, wrapped comfortably in dusty velvet slippers. Horizontally, she was a large woman, but she was vertically challenged, probably no more than four and a half feet tall. Her hair was dyed blonde, but her two-inch long roots told me she was a graying brunette. When she reached the counter, her breasts slid toward me like torpedoes, knocking over a container of business cards.

"Oops, I always do that," she said, smiling at me. "You want a room? How many hours will you be staying?"

"I'm here to pick up two Hispanic women, Rosalba Morales and Juanita Vasquez. Can you tell me which cottage they're in?"

"They're in Cottage Fourteen. Been there two days. You paying for them, too?"

"If their bill hasn't been paid, then I guess I am."

The lady punched some buttons on her cash register. "That will be two hundred twenty dollars."

"Do you take credit cards?"

"Yes, but I have to add five percent for the swipe fee."

I handed her my Visa card.

"That'll be two hundred thirty-one dollars, total, deary." She handed me a slip of paper. "Sign on the line. I'll call them and let them know you're here."

I took the receipt to include in my expense report to French. "Thank you," I replied. Then, I walked back outside to the taxi. "They're in Cottage Fourteen."

My driver followed the parking lot to Cottage Fourteen. As we arrived, the door opened. A woman dressed in tan corduroys and a cotton Aztec top waved at us. Her hair was brown with blond streaks, and she had well-worn flipflops on her feet.

I hopped out. "I'm Bart Jones. Are you Juanita or Rosalba?"

"Rosalba," she said meekly. Then she pointed inside the room. "Juanita there."

She opened the door for me. Juanita was lying on her bed, holding her stomach.

"Is she sick?"

"She start be like that today."

"Help me get her into the car and then we'll come back for your luggage."

We both wrapped one of Juanita's arms around our necks and lifted her. She tried to walk to help us, but she was almost dead weight. Once we got outside the door, I picked her up and carried her in my arms to the car. I tried to look at her eyes, but her head was bent down, her chin resting on her chest.

The driver hopped out and opened the back door for me, and I placed her on the seat. "What's wrong with her?" he asked.

"I haven't the foggiest, but she doesn't have medical insurance so I need to get her back across the border and to my boss, who can handle her medical expenses."

Rosalba brought out the two small backpacks she and Juanita had carried from Mexico. Then the cabby drove us back to Smugglers Hollow.

"Your fare is thirty-six dollars Canadian," he said. "A third of that is idling time."

I didn't quibble with him. I just handed him my Visa card. "Add twenty percent for tip."

He smiled. "When you come back this way again, just tell the operator you want Bobby, and I'll be right around to get you."

"Thanks, Bobby."

Rosalba and I unloaded the two backpacks and Juanita onto a bench outside of the Smugglers Hollow marina. Then I walked into the building. Tonto was sitting at a table drinking a beer.

"You got what you came for, Kemosabe?" he asked.

"I have one more than we bargained for. I'll need to find a cash machine when we get to the other side."

"Two?"

"Yup."

He smiled. He had done nothing extra, and he was getting an additional two hundred dollars from me.

The short bald proprietor overheard me. "If you need a cash machine, there's one against the far wall."

Tonto shook his head at me. "Our bargain was for American currency. We got a cash machine at the

Mohawk Marina."

I nodded. "Sounds good to me. But I could use a hand with the second party. She's sick."

His face dropped. "She's not bringing some kind of contagious disease onto the rez, is she?"

"I hope not, but I've got to get her to a doctor. Come on. She's outside."

Tonto chugged the last third of his beer and then belched as he stood. We walked outside.

"This is Rosalba," I said. "The sick one is Juanita."

Rosalba extended her hand to Tonto. "Ola, Señor."

"Just call me 'Tonto.' "

She giggled.

"What's so funny?"

"You call yourself 'stupid.' "

"Well, I just may be." He looked at me. "Let's load up and get you back across the St. Lawrence."

Tonto and I helped Juanita around the side of the building and onto the docks. We paused for a moment to turn her and then helped her walk down the dock to Tonto's pontoon boat. As we walked, she moaned in discomfort several times.

"Let's put her at the back of the boat," Tonto said as we climbed aboard with Juanita. "If she's carrying something we can catch, I'd rather we left the germs behind us as we head home."

Tonto had a good idea, but if she were contagious, I was sure we would both catch her bug, simply because we had come into contact with her while we helped her to the boat.

I untied the ropes from the cleats on the dock and hopped back onto the boat. Rosalba sat across from me at the front of the boat, her backpacks at her feet. Tonto manned the captain's seat, started the motor, and we were off to the races again.

As our boat blapped across the wakes left by other boats, I could see Juanita turning green. She was probably seasick, but I could do nothing for her. She had not spoken since I first saw her in the motel room. Not even a "thank you" for coming to meet her in Canada.

Rosalba turned her body so she faced into the wind. Her hair blew backward, and I could see a small tattoo of a multicolored parrot on the back of her neck.

She turned to me. "The air, it is so cold and clean. Different from Mexico."

"Si," I replied, forgetting she spoke more English than I spoke Spanish.

"How long we drive after we in America?"

"About five hours if the traffic is light."

She turned and looked at Juanita. "I hope she lives until then."

"Do you know what's wrong with her?"

She nodded. "She swallow something she should not have eaten."

"Did you give her something for her stomach? Maybe an antacid?"

Rosalba shook her head. "She need doctor."

"We can stop at the hospital in Hogansburg. It's a short trip."

Rosalba shook her head. "No hospital. El Escondido has doctor."

She was talking about French. How could she know French had a doctor? I turned and watched as Tonto sped ahead of another freighter. One hundred yards past it, he shot our pontoon boat across its path, and predictably the captain blew his horn. One long blast. Juanita held her hands to her ears.

"She's still alive," I said.

Rosalba nodded and held onto the railing as we lurched across three large wakes left by another freighter. We bounced hard, and I could feel my teeth rattling against each other.

Juanita rolled onto the deck of the boat. When the bouncing stopped, Rosalba and I helped her back onto her seat.

We passed Cornwall Island, and several minutes later Tonto turned to the left and into Mohawk Marina. He coasted the boat gently up to the dock. I hopped out and secured its bow to the dock cleat.

"Are we in USA?" Rosalba asked.

"Not yet. It's just a very short drive away."

"No border patrol? No customs?"

"No. You're safe now."

Tonto cleared his throat and pointed to the Marina Shop. "We need to settle up."

I nodded. "Rosalba, you stay here and watch Juanita. I'll be right back."

Inside, Tonto chatted with two men while I emptied my bank account of two hundred dollars at the cash machine. Then I waved the cash at him and he joined me near the door to the docks.

I handed him the six hundred dollars we had agreed upon. I motioned with my eyes in the direction of the two men with whom he had been chatting. "Friends?"

"Reservation Police. I told them I took a charter party of three out fishing, but the fat woman got seasick, so we had to bring her back in."

I looked back at the men, who seemed uninterested in me, and then back at Tonto. I must have had a concerned look on my face.

"Don't worry," he said. "The New York State Police call this the 'Black Hole' because lots of bad stuff comes across the border here and they catch only two percent of it. But the Reservation Police aren't going to bother you because they saw you paying me money for our fishing trip. Any time a white man gives a Native American money, it's a sign of respect and nobody bothers him. Besides, we were only doing business."

"Can you help me with the 'fat woman?' " I asked.

He smiled. "It's all part of the charter service, and we aim to please."

We walked out the door and back to his pontoon boat. Rosalba lifted the two backpacks onto her shoulder, and Tonto and I held Juanita up while she attempted to walk. It was like trying to guide a drunk, and I was exhausted by the time we reached my Bronco.

I unlocked the doors. Rosalba threw the backpacks into the rear compartment and then climbed into the front seat. We laid Juanita on the back seat, which was probably the most comfortable way for her to ride, even if it was in violation of the new backseat seatbelt law. Then I shook Tonto's hand.

"I wish I knew your name and address so I could send you a 'thank you' note."

"It's 'Tonto,' Kemosabe."

I understood confidentiality was of utmost importance.

"So, if I ever need another boat ride to Canada, how do I find you?"

"Just call Mohawk Marina and ask for the phone number of the guy who plays chicken with the freighters. They'll give you my number and tell you to ask for

'Tonto.' "

I laughed. "Thank you again, Tonto."

Chapter Twenty

I hustled back to Willow Falls without stopping for dinner or a bathroom break. Rosalba slept the entire way, her head wedged between the edge of her seat and the windowpane of the passenger's side door. Juanita survived the trip, too, occasionally reminding me she was lying in the back seat by moaning in a guttural growl, somewhat like a tomcat during mating season. Her life must have been hell for the entire trip.

When we were half an hour away, I broke the law again by calling French while I drove.

"Ola, Caesar, it's me. I have your packages."

"Good. When can I expect delivery?"

"About half an hour. We've got a problem, however."

"What's the matter?"

"One of them is very sick. I don't know what's wrong. The other one told me she ate something which didn't agree with her."

"Can I speak with her?"

"She's horizontal in the back seat, only semi-conscious."

"I'll have a doctor here when you arrive. Don't park out front, but come directly into the truck repair warehouse, okay?"

"Yeah. Tell the guards at the front gate to expect me."

"They'll be waiting for you."

****

When I pulled up to the gate at Cabrillo Construction at seven in the evening, the two guards stepped aside and waved me through, one with his hand and the other with the barrel of an Uzi which was tucked under his arm. French had fulfilled his promise.

I followed the tarmac to the truck repair warehouse, where I found the door to its large bay wide open. I pulled in and parked behind a black Mercedes, my tires squealing on the smooth concrete surface as I skidded to a stop. I saw motion in the shadows and realized it was French and a middle-aged man with salt and pepper hair who was dressed in a business suit.

I tapped Rosalba on her shoulder. "We're here."

She raised her head and rubbed her eyes. "Where is 'here?'"

"Cabrillo Construction. Caesar French is here."

She sat up quickly and ran her fingers through her hair. "Is okay?"

"Yes."

My door opened and French looked in. "Hello, Rosalba," he said, looking past me.

"Ola, Señor."

"Where is my patient?" the man behind French asked.

I looked beyond French's face and my eyes met the stranger's. "In the back seat."

He opened the back door and then closed it, realizing Juanita's head was best reached by the rear door on the passenger's side. A few moments later, that door opened. I looked over the front seat and watched as he listened to her heart with a stethoscope and then

136

pulled up her eyelids so he could see the whites of her eyes and her pupils.

He said something to Rosalba in Spanish. She replied. He said something else. She shook her head and then nodded as she replied. Of course, I could not understand anything which had transpired, but I could see her eyes welling with tears.

The doctor stood and said something to French over the roof of the Bronco. French replied and then he shouted something to a group of men. Two came running to my Bronco and helped Juanita out. One of them scooped her into his arms and followed the doctor into the warehouse's office area.

Rosalba got out of my Bronco and removed the two backpacks from the rear cargo area. She walked up to French, kissed his right hand, and said something else I could not understand, except, "Gracias." I supposed she was grateful to him for helping her out of some bad situation in Mexico.

French put his arm around her and walked her into the office area. I was not certain if that was my signal to go home, so I waited for a few minutes, just to be sure.

When French reappeared from the office area, he seemed upset.

"Is Juanita okay?" I asked.

"The doctor is not happy with her condition. He feels she belongs in the hospital, but I can't send her there because if I do, she'll be arrested."

"Is she wanted for something?"

"No, but she is carrying something which could send her to jail."

I put two and two together. She ate something which did not agree with her. She could be arrested for carrying it. "Is she a mule?"

"Unfortunately, yes. My corporate superior took advantage of my sending the ladies airplane tickets by shipping me something to sell. He expects the proceeds of its sale to be returned to him in one month. This is a problem for me."

I was not sure what the product was, but for me there was little doubt it was heroin, cocaine, methamphetamine, or some concoction of two or more illicit substances. "Mules" are people who carry the drugs across the border, most often inside their bodies, where the contraband cannot be detected by dogs at the border. Most often the drugs are placed into condoms, which are then knotted. The extra rubber is cut away, leaving a pellet the size of a jawbreaker. Mules coat the pellets with olive oil and then swallow them whole, often carrying as many as forty-five or fifty inside themselves as they travel. When they reach their destinations, they pass the pellets through normal bodily functions. The recipients rinse the pellets, dry them, and then cut them open to remove the product for sale. Sometimes mules undergo surgery where large packages of drugs are inserted into their abdomens. Once they have safely crossed the border, they undergo a second surgery, where the packaged drugs are removed. In either scenario, if the pellets or packages leak while inside the body, the mule often dies of a drug overdose. I assumed Juanita was suffering from a leaky container.

I rubbed my forehead with my right hand. "So, I've been an unwitting accomplice in a drug smuggling scheme?"

"It looks that way, Jones. I never would have asked you to go get the ladies if I had suspected they were carrying contraband. But I think you are safe from suspicion."

"Well, I'm not safe from your war with Onondaga."

He cocked his head, looking for an explanation.

"Like I told you yesterday, the other night my cabin was shot up by a bunch of guys driving an orange pickup. It's almost totally destroyed."

"You reported it to the police?"

"Yes, but I haven't told the cabin's owner yet. I've already had the insurance adjuster out to look at it, and he should give me the bad news soon."

"You might want to think about moving. Once you fix it up, they'll be back. They know who you are now, and they know you work for me."

The door to the office area opened, and the doctor walked out. His white shirt was tucked angrily into grey suit slacks. "I can't continue to do this, Caesar," he blurted boldly.

French gestured to me with an open hand. "Dr. Blankenship, this is my chief investigator, Bart Jones."

The doctor nodded at me and then focused upon French. "These women have ingested pellets of illegal drugs. I've given both of them a laxative to accelerate their elimination processes, but unless we get the sick one to the hospital, I cannot be responsible for her well-being."

"Do you know what drugs are in the pellets?"

"No, but I've drawn a blood sample from the sick one. What's her name?"

"Juanita," I said.

The doctor looked at me. "Thank you." He turned back to French. "If she dies, Juanita's death will be on your hands, Caesar."

French nodded. His eyes descended to the floor.

"I can't continue to provide medical services to you and your staff outside the county's medical system, especially if it might implicate me in drug smuggling or human trafficking. I have my reputation and my medical license to consider."

"My concern for the moment is for these unfortunate ladies, Francisco. Will you at least stay here with them through the night?" French asked.

"If either one dies, I am going to have to report the death to the authorities, Caesar."

"If you must…"

The doctor held up a vial of blood. "Meanwhile, do you have a runner who can take this blood sample to the hospital? It will give us valuable information: what drug is in her system, how toxic she is, and what we can use to counter its effects."

"I'll take it," I said. "Should I ask to speak with a specific lab assistant?"

Dr. Blankenship handed me the vial. "Nobody specific. The tube has my contact information on it, and they'll call me when they have the diagnosis. Ask them to expedite it."

I bade both gentlemen farewell and drove directly to the emergency entrance of Willow Falls General Hospital. I parked in "family and friends" parking and walked inside with the vial.

An elderly woman in a pin-striped dress looked up as I came in.

"May I help you?"

"Yes, I'm bringing a vial of blood for the lab from Dr. Blankenship. It's an emergency job."

She picked up her telephone and dialed a three-digit

extension. "I have a gentleman here with a request for emergency lab work." She drummed the eraser end of her pencil on the table-top blotter. After half a minute, she nodded. "Okay, I'll send him right down."

She pointed at a swinging door at the end of the room. "Go through the door and follow the red line on the wall until you come to the lab. Ask for Roxanne."

I followed the receptionist's directions and found the lab two turns and a hallway away from the emergency room. I knocked on the door and was greeted by a young woman in a lab coat with a black hijab on her head.

"I'm looking for Roxanne," I said.

She turned and looked behind her. "Roxy, it's for you."

"Thanks. I am expecting a man with—" She stopped speaking when she saw me. "Detective, how nice to see you."

I fought to place her face and then realized who she was. "Well, Roxanne Windsor, what's a fantastic real estate salesperson like you doing in a medical lab?"

Helen Martin and I had interrogated Roxanne at least twice during our investigation of the sanguinarian cult six months ago. Roxanne was known as "the Queen from England" during blood drinking rituals, but we couldn't pin anything on her that would stick, so she was never arrested or charged with a crime. Besides, she gave us valuable information which helped us to solve the case. It would have been a travesty to arrest her for some small crime.

"I work here evenings to supplement my home sales income. Home sales have been down this year, so the regular money comes in handy."

"Besides, you get to handle a lot of blood."

She smiled. "Yes, my knowledge of blood has come in handy, but they hired me because of my past experience as an emergency medical staffer in England. I was young then, but the ambulance experience added to my resume."

"Well, I'm happy to see you're still living stateside."

"Yes, me too. I passed my citizenship exams and am expecting to be sworn in next month."

"Excellent." Then I changed the subject. "Listen, Roxanne, I have a vial of blood which may contain some illegal substances. Dr. Blankenship needs to know what he's dealing with. It's a life and death situation. Can you expedite it?"

"Sure. We'll get right on it." She turned to the Arabic woman. "Fatma, we need to run a toxicology series on this blood sample.'

Fatma took the sample, read the label, and asked, "Are you going to wait or does the doctor want us to call?"

"He'd like an immediate call, please."

While Fatma began the analysis, Roxanne touched my arm. "We'll have to do dinner sometime, Detective."

"Just call me Bart, Roxanne. I've left the police department."

"Really? What are you up to now?"

"Private investigation. It's the same field, but a little less restrictive."

"Then we really *must* do dinner. How about this Saturday?"

I had nothing on my calendar, and she looked especially attractive in a lab coat. "Sure, if you don't mind being seen with an ex-detective. Do you mind riding in an old Bronco?"

She didn't look excited about being seen in my ride, but she scribbled an address and a cell phone number on the back of her business card. "Pick me up at seven and wear a tie. I'll make us reservations."

"Where are we going?"

"It's a surprise, but you'll like it."

I bid her farewell until Saturday and then headed back to Mariaville Lake and home-sweet-holey-home. It had been a long day and I was looking forward to some shuteye.

Chapter Twenty-One

Loud banging on my front door roused me from sleep at eight in the morning.

"Hold your horses," I shouted. I pulled on my pants and threw on a sweatshirt.

I walked into the kitchen and looked through a bullet hole in the front door. I didn't recognize the guy, but he looked upset. I unlocked the door and opened it.

He barged into the kitchen. "Jeezuz H…what did you do to our camp?"

He was in his mid-thirties, muscular, with wild blue eyes. His crew cut was fresh with sharp edges, and he wore a Schenectady fireman's wind breaker and ballcap.

"Who are you?" I asked.

"Carl. Carl Astor. My family owns this camp, or what's left of it. My dad said he was letting a cop stay in it for the winter, but he didn't say you'd destroy it."

"I'm Bart Jones, the cop your dad let stay here. This mess just happened. It was shot up two days ago. I've been out of town since then and haven't had the chance to call your dad, but it's on my agenda today. I've already had the damages appraised and should get the repair estimate sometime today."

"This is no repair job. It's a total rebuild. Nothing has been left undamaged."

"I think it was Los Cuernos. They used full metal jacket rounds, probably three-oh-eights, and it's pretty obvious they were trying to kill me."

"When my dad sees this mess, you're going to wish they had."

I knew Carl was right. Joey Astor was a nice man, but the camp had been in his wife's family for more than forty years and she was emotionally attached to it. She would never forgive him for letting me stay here, even it could be fully restored and upgraded. The camp of her childhood was now history. She would be outraged, and Joey would catch the full force of her fury. No doubt, he would pass it along to me.

"You stopped by unannounced. Were you looking for anything in particular?" I asked.

"A neighbor called to alert me our camp was in shambles. I came by to see for myself. It's worse than I ever thought it could be."

"Well, you should inspect every room. You'll see I was lucky to walk out of here alive after the attack. If I had been in bed when they opened fire, right now I'd be getting my face painted at the mortician's."

"My folks are going to be very upset when they see what's happened."

"You don't owe me anything, but as one public servant to another, I'm asking you to let me call your father and tell him myself. I'd like to clean up the remainder of the shattered glass and wood debris before he comes to see this mess. It'll be safer for him, and for your mother if she accompanies him."

Carl walked into every room, his footsteps accentuated by the sounds of tiny pieces of glass breaking under the weight of his boots. When he returned to the kitchen, the look on his face reaffirmed how serious the damage was.

"Well, are you going to call your father this morning, or are you going to let me call him?" I asked.

"I'll let you call him. I don't want him to think I was prying around in his business. But you'd better do it today."

"Thanks, Carl. You can count on it."

Before he walked outside, Carl turned back toward me. "Who's your insurance agent?"

"State Farm. Their adjuster is supposed to call me with the estimate today."

"Did you get homeowners' or renters' insurance?"

"Renters."

"Because you're not the owner, they're just going to cover your material possessions. I've seen it a dozen times with apartment fires and floods. Damage to the camp will fall on my father's policy." He paused a moment. "I hope to God he renewed it."

****

I called Helen.

" 'Bout time you called," she said. "I was beginning to think you didn't love me no more."

"Don't you use a maid service?"

"Sure do. A lady with my nails don't need to break them by doing manual labor."

"Can you give me the number? I have a bit of an emergency clean-up job."

"It's gonna cost you. How about dinner tonight? My place. I'm making spaghetti."

I really didn't want to negotiate for a simple phone number. I had had Helen's spaghetti once before. She had loaded the sauce with habanero peppers, which was a real turn-off to me. But I didn't want to offend her. I owed Helen a lot and we were friends, even though I had

146

not seen much of her since going out on rip.

"Sure. What time?"

"Come around seven. We'll eat at seven thirty."

"How about that phone number?"

****

The insurance adjuster called me at ten thirty. "This is Brewster Smith. Mr. Jones, the damage to the property was extensive, and you only have renter's insurance. The home office needs a list of all your personal items destroyed or badly damaged in the gunfight."

"It wasn't a gunfight. It was an assault with intent to kill a police officer."

"Well, whatever. I still need a list of all your things which were damaged or destroyed and their replacement cost. You got five hundred dollars deductible, and the company will cover the remainder."

"It'll be a couple of days. I'll call you when I have it."

I needed time to confer with Joey Astor and I needed to review my policy to see how much personal property coverage I had. If Joey did not have full insurance coverage on the property, I planned to claim I rented an empty cabin and all the furniture and appliances were mine. Yeah, it would be insurance fraud, but who was going to argue with two police officers?

****

I dialed Joey Astor's cell phone and was directed to his message box. So, I left a message.

"Joey, this is Bart Jones. I've got a major problem to share with you, and you won't be happy about it. Call me when you have a few minutes to chat."

Joey returned my call within two minutes.

"What's the problem, Bart?"

"Your cabin has been shot up. You're going to need to call your insurance claims office and get an adjuster over as soon as possible."

"What? You're kidding me, ain't ya? Who put you up to this?"

"I sure wish I was kidding, but I'm not. It happened two nights ago. Orange pickup truck with several men firing semiautomatic weapons. State police think they were steel jacket three-oh-eights. Maybe close to a hundred rounds through the siding. Just about everything has a bullet hole in it. All your glass has been blown out. Some rounds went in one side of the cabin and out the other."

"Now I know you're kidding. Is this April Fool's Day? Ha ha!"

"This is no B.S., Joey. Maybe you ought to meet me out there after work...and be sure to bring your insurance adjuster."

"If you're not making some kind of stupid joke, Rosemarie is gonna be really upset. Who the heck would shoot up an old cabin out in the woods?"

"I'm not sure. I'm thinking it was Los Cuernos. That's what I told the State Trooper who answered the call."

"Los Cuernos? Did you aggravate one of them or something?"

"Looks that way. Can you meet me at the cabin this afternoon around five?"

"Yeah, I guess so. I won't tell Rosemarie until after I see it first."

"That's probably smart. Maybe you can break the news to her gently."

"Maybe I can ease her pain a little if I break

something on you, too."

****

Joey showed up at four-forty-five. He was fifteen minutes early, but I was ready for him. I had used his father-in-law's ancient ShopVac to clean up all the floors and area rugs, and then I had washed and waxed the kitchen and bathroom floors on my hands and knees. The place sparkled—well, as much as it could with plastic stapled across all the windows, holes through the exterior walls, and the appliances dimpled and perforated by bullets.

Joey's expression told me the camp's condition was worse than he had anticipated, although I thought I had given him enough warning about what to expect. I mean, I did tell him to expect more than a hundred bullet holes and no glass in the windows.

"Jeezus H.," he said, using the same term his son had used. His jaw dropped in shock. "They really *were* trying to kill you."

"I hope Rosemarie sees it that way. There was nothing I could do about it. When the shooting started, all I could do was roll onto the floor and pray their aim was high."

We walked around the house, inspecting the exterior damage before venturing inside.

"All the lakeside holes splinter outwards, toward the water," he said.

"Yeah, I think they passed straight through the cabin."

"You still got some glass in the cracks between the boards on the deck. I imagine there's some in the grass. Nobody had better go barefoot this summer."

I nodded in agreement.

We could not open the sliding glass doors because of the plywood I had screwed over the gaping holes which remained when the glass collapsed, so we walked back to the kitchen door and went inside. As we did, another car pulled into the gravel parking area.

"That's probably Mark Gratton. He's with Gratton Insurance."

I had heard of the Gratton Insurance Agency, a small firm in Schenectady which offered insurance of all kinds from multiple national chains. When a client asked for a specific type of insurance, Gratton would ask for quotes from half a dozen companies, and then recommend the best deal to his client. In return, the company which won the contract paid him a commission for his work.

We heard the car door slam shut. "Woowee!" the driver exclaimed. "You got some major damage all right."

Joey walked outside and greeted Gratton. I followed him outside.

"This here is Bart Jones," Joey said. "He was the target."

I shook Gratton's hand. He was in his late forties, bald, and wore horn-rimmed glasses with thick lenses. His short-sleeved pinstriped shirt was stained where his belly protruded from beneath his ribs. I thought it was obvious the red Peugeot he drove was the only thing that might attract a woman. Maybe.

"Did you set fireworks off inside?" he asked with a smile. His teeth were crooked.

"There might have been less damage if I had," I replied.

"Who put plastic on the windows?" he asked.

"I did," I said. "It was a quick fix until you and Joey

could get here."

"Well, that's good. That'll save us some money in materials and labor. And it'll keep the insects and critters out."

He raised his clipboard and made some notes. "You got a police report?"

"You'll have to get it from the State Police," I replied. "The name of the trooper who wrote the report is Nathan Walker."

"I know Nate," Gratton said. "He's a good man…thorough. I'll call him in the morning and get a copy for Allegiant."

Joey turned to me. "That's my insurance company."

I nodded. I had already figured out what Gratton meant.

I waited outside while Gratton and Joey inspected the damage inside. I could hear them chatting as they spotted damages. When they emerged, Gratton was holding a camera and his clipboard in his left hand while writing on his third sheet of notebook paper with his right.

"What do you think?" Joey asked.

Gratton reviewed his notes. "You might want to tear it down and build something new. Of course, that's up to the adjusters at Allegiant. I've seen them declare places with less damage 'total losses.' "

Gratton took some pictures of the exterior, and then shook Joey's hand. "You should be hearing from me in a couple of days. Then, regardless of the outcome, you're going to have to get a couple of contractors out here to give you quotes on repair or demolition."

Joey nodded. "Thanks, Mark. Give Belinda my regards."

Gratton started his car and headed back to the main road.

"He thinks it's a total," Joey said. "Rosemarie won't be happy with that, but I think you might have done me a favor."

"Really?"

"Yeah. You gotta admit this place was in need of some repair and face-lifting. I don't know who did the plumbing and wiring, but it was probably her father and he didn't follow any of the construction codes. He probably never even got a Certificate of Occupancy. And God only knows what the ants and mice might have done to the infrastructure over the years."

I nodded. "I don't think they had construction codes and C.O.'s back in the fifties. At least not out here."

"Yeah. It would be nice to vacation in something new, with no repairs nagging at us. Rosemarie actually might look at this event as a blessing. Besides, if the insurance company pays for it, it won't cost us anything. She'll like that."

"Let's hope."

Chapter Twenty-Two

On my way to Helen's, I stopped at Tony's Fine Wine and Liquors and bought a bottle of Chianti, thinking it might go well with spaghetti. I arrived at Helen's home at seven and pulled in behind her Hyundai. Her rear license plate was dented in the middle. I wondered if she recently had been rear-ended or had backed into something which was harder than her bumper. If it were anything important, it would come up in the evening's conversation.

I was surprised when Helen's mother, Momma Gracie, met me at the door. She squeezed my cheeks with both hands and kissed me on my nose. "Where you been keepin' yourself, Jonesy? My little girl's been missing you."

"I've parted ways with the police department, Momma."

"I know. Helen told me all about it. They almost let her go, too, but she was just high enough on the list to miss the cut. She's a lucky girl."

"The department is the lucky one. If they had let Helen go, they wouldn't have had a detective worth the salary they pay him. Helen does the work of two men…maybe three…and she's never left a case unsolved."

"Yeah, I have," Helen chimed in, wiping her hands on a small towel as she walked into the living room from the kitchen. "I haven't solved the murders of those two headless horsemen from Mariaville Lake."

I greeted Helen with a friendly hug and a peck on the cheek. "Me neither. If I had, you'd have been the first to know."

The three of us walked into the kitchen, where Helen handed me a corkscrew. "Get busy opening the bottle of Chianti. Dinner's almost ready."

I twisted the corkscrew into the bottle's plastic cork and tugged on it. It did not budge. Momma Gracie stood back while I placed the bottle between my legs and pulled with all my might. "Damn, that thing's in there like King Arthur's sword."

Helen opened a cabinet and set a box on the countertop. "Try this new-fangled thing. I got it for Christmas from Cousin Sammy."

It was a device which injects carbon dioxide into the bottle through a needle, building pressure until the cork pops out. I followed the directions and eventually watched the cork slide out as though it were greased. "How's that for smacking down my masculinity. I've got to get one of these."

Momma Gracie handed me three glasses. "Well, let's pour some of that expensive stuff and see if we like it."

I poured three half-glasses of wine and handed one each to Helen and her mom. "To friendship," I said.

We touched glasses and tasted the Chianti.

"Not too bad," Momma Gracie said.

"You should have brought two bottles, Jonesy," Helen added. "When the wine's gone, we'll have to drink beer."

Helen moved us into her dining room and served

dinner, scooping spaghetti from a large tureen in which she had mixed the macaroni with the sauce. In a separate bowl she offered meatballs, the pre-made kind which are the size of ping pong balls and perfectly round. "Jonesy, do you want hot pepper? I didn't put any in the sauce this time because it upsets Momma's tummy."

I thanked God for small favors. "Nope. This looks great just the way it is."

And it wasn't bad. I had had worse, including the sauce Helen made the last time she served me spaghetti. Maybe she thought I liked it, though I would have preferred a steak or a meatloaf. But beggars can't be choosey, and I was as close to a beggar as an employed man could be.

We were halfway through dinner when Momma Gracie started playing thirty questions with me— "Where were you born, Jonesy?" "Where did you go to high school…college?" "You got any hobbies?" "Have any children?" "What happened between you and your wife?" "Dating anybody?"

Finally, Helen broke the chain. "Seen anything of the Queen from England?"

"Roxanne Windsor?"

"Yeah, that's the one."

"Yeah, actually. I bumped into her at Willow Falls General. She works as a technician in the blood lab."

"Ha, that's a good one. She probably drinks a quart of their samples every day."

"She invited me out to dinner…sort of a noncommittal date for some time in the future. Strange, isn't she?"

"Well, I got some new skinny on her. She's started a local chapter of the Black Hat Society. Of course, as the founding member, she's the queen."

I had never heard of the organization. It sounded kind of uppity. "What's the Black Hat Society? Sounds like a bunch of morticians."

"You're pretty close. Actually, the Society is a group of witches, and every local chapter has its own purpose. Some are into the Satanic thing, while others are into community service. You know, bad witches versus good witches, like in *The Wizard of Oz*."

"They all sound bad, if you ask me," Momma Gracie said.

"That's okay, Momma. Think about the good witch in the television show you used to watch...wasn't her name Samantha?"

Momma Gracie nodded. "Yeah, I guess she was a good one."

Helen turned her attention back to me. "Once you get by the blood tasting stuff, Roxanne's group is into community service."

"Really?"

"Yeah. Recently the Department called on her group to help solve the two murders which we're both working on."

"The two men found at Mariaville Lake?"

Helen stuffed a fork full of meatball into her mouth and then she nodded.

"What did they learn?" I asked.

"Apparently they did a séance and called on the souls of the two departed men to tell the witches who killed them. Roxanne wants to meet to go over what they learned. She says it is interesting but puzzling."

"So, when are you meeting her?"

"Tomorrow at noon in the hospital cafeteria. It's her

lunch hour."

"Can I come?"

"I hoped you would."

****

Helen and I arrived at the hospital at eleven fifty and found the cafeteria by asking directions at the Information Desk. Roxanne met us at the door at five minutes past noon. She looked like any other employee, dressed in light green scrubs and white athletic shoes with non-skid soles. Her auburn hair was pulled back into a ponytail, which made her look younger than her age, which I guessed was thirty-eight or nine.

I bought each of us a cup of coffee and then we found an empty table near the door. People were beginning to flow into the room like it was lunchtime, which, of course, it was. Our table sported a plastic surface which resembled the hospital's white and gray terrazzo floors. The screws which held its aluminum framing in place were rusted, probably from the heavy bleach solution the hospital used when cleaning it to keep a variety of viruses from spreading.

"So nice to see both of you again," Roxanne said, "especially you, Mr. Jones. I was disappointed to learn you left the police department. I hope it was your decision and not theirs."

"We had a mutual parting of the ways, Ms. Windsor."

"Didn't I already give you permission to call me Roxanne? I wish you would."

"Sure, Roxanne."

"So, has your Black Hat Society accomplished its task?" Helen asked, getting to the point of our visit.

"It took longer than I thought it would, but many of

our group are new to the process and lack the concentration skills necessary to ferret out all the details you are seeking."

"What did you learn?"

"Well, as you requested, we focused on the deaths of the two Hispanic men. We managed to contact both during a séance, though one was less able to communicate with us than the other. It may have been the language barrier."

"How about the fact they were dead? Did that have anything to do with it?" I asked.

"Now don't be such a skeptic, Mr. Jones. Bear with me while I give you the details."

"Go on, please," Helen said.

Roxanne took a sip of her coffee. "Ugh. This is the worst coffee in the world. What do they say? 'Waiter, waiter, my coffee tastes like dirt. That's strange, sir, it was only ground yesterday.' "

Helen and I both smiled at the old joke.

Roxanne put three packets of sugar and two containers of cream into her cup of coffee and then stirred it vigorously.

"As I was saying…what we learned was both men were killed by the same individual whom they told us is 'a snake in human form.' "

I smiled. Helen rolled her eyes at me.

"You must find the snake," Roxanne said.

"Sure," I replied with a snicker. "We'll look for someone with scaley skin, slits for eyes, and a forked tongue."

"Exactly, so to speak," Roxanne replied. "The spirits talk to us in metaphors and symbols."

She took a sip of coffee. Her expression told us her

coffee still tasted rank. I tasted mine. Yup, it was definitely bad.

Roxanne placed her hand on mine. "Spirits don't use words when they speak to us. They impress images and feelings into our brains. Our task is to decipher their meaning."

'So, you expect us to figure out what they mean?" Helen asked.

"Yes, the spirits were very clear about that. You are supposed to 'look for the snake among the discarded of the people of the hills.' "

"The capital region is surrounded by hilly geography, Roxanne. The spirits sent you a bogus message." I looked at Helen. "I hope you didn't pay too much for this malarky."

Roxanne shot me a look of disappointment. "Come now, Mr. Jones. I've already deciphered one part of the message."

"And what would that be?"

"The 'people of the hills' refers to your native Americans…the indigenous."

"And the 'snake'?" Helen asked.

"I'm still uncertain, but I'm working on it. You have to concentrate on the images and feelings you get when you think about the term. Don't think of its denotation. What does the word 'snake' connote within you?"

I had to think about that.

Roxanne looked at her cell phone. "They need me back at the lab."

"Thanks so much for your time, Roxanne," Helen said. "If you can think of anything else or if you decipher any more of the message from the séance, please give me a call."

"Will do, detective."

Roxanne stood and shook our hands. Then she disappeared into the swarm of people in the hallway.

Helen and I carried our three cups of coffee to the dishwashing station and handed them to a young woman who was wearing a hair net and a large white apron. Only Roxanne's cup showed evidence someone had drunk from it. Then we found the exit and left the hospital.

Back in the car, I pulled out my cell phone and tapped "people of the hills" into its internet search engine. Instantly the internet told me the term referred to "the Onondaga Nation."

"No surprise there," I said aloud.

"What did you find out, Jonesy?" Helen asked.

"I think 'the snake' may be an employee of Onondaga Trash Company. The word 'Onondaga' means 'people of the hills.' "

"You're starting to scare me, Jonesy. You're already starting to think like that Roxanne weirdo."

"Who asked Roxanne to conduct a séance with her Black Hat Society?"

Helen looked at me sheepishly.

"Then don't give me any B.S. about thinking like Roxanne." I replied. "I didn't ask her for any witchy help in solving this case. Are you practicing voodoo, Helen?"

"So, should we be looking for a native-American?" she asked, ignoring my comment.

"Roxanne said to look 'among the discarded of the people of the hills.' That could mean someone who has been excommunicated from the Onondaga Tribe or it could mean among the discarded items—the trash—of the Onondaga Tribe. But I'm betting it means 'Onondaga Trash Company.' "

"Now you're starting to sound like Sherlock Holmes, Jonesy. But I'll bet you're right."

"Me, too."

I smiled at Helen. "You got any friends or contacts at Onondaga Trash?"

"I don't think so, but I'll check around the department."

"I may have access to the sister of one of the machos who works there. I'll tell you what I find out."

Helen changed the subject. "Jonesy, how's that place of yours? I heard it was shot up. You need a place to stay? I got room if you need one."

I would have taken Helen up on her offer, except her mother had been pushing her to date me. Heck, she had been pushing me to date Helen, too. I think Momma Gracie was hoping we'd enter a sleeping relationship and eventually tie the knot. I really liked Helen, but somewhere deep inside me was a warning from my father: "Don't shit where you eat, son." What he meant was workplace relationships eventually go sour, forcing one of the partners to leave the job. Okay, so I was no longer working at the police department, but I was still in a working relationship with Helen and if I mixed work with a sexual relationship, I would be setting the work relationship up for a shit show, if you know what I mean. And lately, I had been good at orchestrating shit shows.

Chapter Twenty-Three

Brewster Smith called me at eight thirty in the morning. "I got the estimate from your insurance company," he said.

"So how much are they giving me?"

"That depends. They asked me to be sure about the contents of the domicile. You know, which items belonged to you and which ones came with the property.

"Like I told you," I lied, "the place was empty. I had to furnish it completely, including buying all the appliances. You included the propane grill on the deck, didn't you? I'll admit I bought a lot of the stuff second hand, but it was all mine, what's left of it."

"That's what I told them. They want to know if you can provide receipts of purchase."

"What do you think? Who keeps receipts, anyway?"

"That's what I told them, too. I explained you are a cop and somebody you arrested tried to get you killed."

"Good. Thank you. So, what's the payout for replacement furnishings?"

"They've reduced the replacement value to used items, instead of new. In the end, you're going to see only seventeen thousand five hundred dollars."

I wanted to do a backflip, but I could not let Brewster know I was floored by the amount I was getting for the junk Joey's father-in-law had used to furnish the cabin. "Jeez," I said, "couldn't you push them for a little more? It's going to be hard to refurnish this place with only seventeen thousand."

"Seventeen thousand five hundred," he repeated, as though the additional five hundred would buy more than a basic television set.

"Well, I guess it will have to do. When should I expect the check?"

"They'll have it in the mail today, so you should see it no later than next Tuesday."

"Thanks for all your help, Brewster."

"Sure thing. Happy to be of service to you."

We hung up, and for a brief moment I wondered if my bogus claim would ever be found out. For example, would the two insurance companies — mine and Joey Astor's — ever compare notes and demand return of the money I had received for the furniture and appliances which belonged to Joey? I didn't worry for too long, however. I had things to do. Besides, recently I had smuggled two illegal aliens into the country and at least one of them was carrying illegal drugs, which made me an accomplice to drug smuggling. What's a little insurance fraud when added to those crimes?

****

At ten o'clock in the morning I drove into Willow Falls and stopped at Cabrillo Construction. The main gate was still barricaded, but the security guards recognized my Bronco and waved me through without stopping me. It was nice to be one of the crowd, even if the crowd was an army of new Americans from a bunch of third-world countries.

"Good to see you, Jones," Caesar said when I came into the main office. He was leaning over his secretary, Laverne, reading something she had typed into her computer. Both of them were wearing bulletproof vests, though Caesar's body seemed better suited to it than Laverne's. Because of her endowment, the top edges of her vest would not come together, and any shot near the solar plexus area would probably result in a life-ending wound.

"I was hoping you'd bring me up to speed on the delivery I made last week," I said.

"Let's go into my office." Caesar patted Laverne on her shoulder. "Just do what we discussed, and everything should be fine."

She nodded and started typing.

French opened the door to the work area and ushered me through. I waited at his office door until he caught up with me. He used a key to unlock it and we went in. Hanging on the wall beside his desk was a sawed-off pump shotgun. I assumed he was prepared for the possibility of trouble.

"How have you been?" he asked as he sat down. "Coffee?"

I sat in the chair across from him. "No, I think I've had enough this morning."

"It's for the best. I'm all out of the good stuff, but I am expecting another shipment next week. Sombrero Negro brand. It's a dark roast Colombian."

"Save me a cup."

He laughed. "So, you're here about Juanita and Rosalba?"

"I've been very worried about Juanita. I thought she was going to die in my car on the ride from Canada to Willow Falls."

"Another hour or two and she would have. Fortunately, Dr. Blankenship is a very talented man. He gave her something to counteract the drugs, and then he performed emergency surgery on her and retrieved all forty condoms from her stomach. One was leaking small amounts of powder into her system. She was very lucky to have survived the flight to Canada. She should be out of rehab in a month."

"Rehab? Why is she there?"

"It's a precaution. Dr. Blankenship says some of these new synthetic drugs are more addictive than cocaine or heroin. Maybe ten times as addictive. In rehab she'll get the care she needs."

"And Rosalba?"

"She's fine and living with her brother in Schenectady. Dr. Blankenship gave her the liquid you are given for a rectal anal exam."

"Do you mean for a colonoscopy?"

"Yes, that's the stuff. The stuff you drink to prepare for the exam…you know, to clean you out. She drank it and dropped forty-three condoms into the bucket."

"What were they carrying? Cocaine? Heroin?"

"Dr. Blankenship isn't sure. It was heroin cut with some new chemical. I've sent Pancho Villa to Sinaloa to find out what it is."

"Pancho Villa?"

"His real name is Joseph Arango, but he is a descendent of Pancho Villa and wears the same moustache. I've sent him to Sinaloa to find out what's in that stuff and to take a message to my immediate superior, a gentleman who likes to be called 'La Cabra.' "

"I'm sure you're not happy with how he treated those women."

"And how he put me directly at risk of arrest for

human trafficking and drug smuggling. Nobody does that to me."

"If your message angers him, I hope your superior doesn't take it out on Pancho Villa."

"I see you know something about human nature, my friend. La Cabra certainly can be that way. So can his men. I hope Pancho Villa successfully delivers the message I sent. If he does and if he does not escape alive, I am a dead man. One word from Sinaloa and someone here who has loyalty to La Cabra will be sure I disappear quickly and my body is never found."

I didn't like hearing what French was telling me. He had let his ego take control of his response to his superior and potentially had put everyone here at Cabrillo Construction in harm's way, including me.

"You've made me afraid for you," I said.

"But this is business, my friend, and that bastard unnecessarily risked the lives of two innocent women who were coming to the U.S. under my protection. And in doing so, he put me and this entire international human rescue mission at risk. He deserves to die."

A popping sound erupted in the repair shop area of the warehouse. Then the sounds of men shouting.

French opened a cabinet and handed me a bulletproof vest. "Put this on. Onondaga is here."

While French stuffed three additional shells into his shotgun, I quickly donned the military green Kevlar vest and pulled my forty-five from its position in my belt at the small of my back. I clicked the safety off and followed Caesar into the hallway and in the direction of the firefight.

When we entered the open warehouse, we could see flames leaping toward the ceiling from a dozen boxes which had been stacked near the building's interior wall. Another line of fire, with flames at least four feet high, extended for fifty feet and out the warehouse door.

"Here it comes again," someone shouted.

"Derribarlo!" another man shouted.

"What did he say?" I shouted at French.

"Shoot it down."

"Airborne? Is it an airborne assault?"

"I think so. We hadn't planned for that."

Suddenly the air erupted with the sound of several small electric engines. I looked up as men began shooting into the air at a six-foot square aluminum drone with four rotors. Hanging below it was some sort of device and below that was a video camera.

"Shoot it, Caesar," I shouted. "You have a shotgun. Our pistols and rifles are no match for a flying object."

French shot twice at it. Bang! Bang! The device stopped in midair and turned toward him. Pellets of fire dropped from the container which protruded above the camera.

"Run, Caesar," I shouted. "It's a flame thrower."

French fired a third round at the drone and then ran toward the hallway to his office. The drone let fly a stream of burning liquid which followed at his heels but never reached him. French disappeared into the hallway. Behind him a path of fire danced wildly on the concrete floor.

The drone turned toward a parked trash truck and floated to it. I fired six rounds at the drone, missing it every time. Instead, my bullets punched dents into the warehouse's steel roof. As the drone unleashed its stream of fire toward the truck, one of Caesar's men ran beneath the drone and emptied the clip of an AK-47 at it: Bap!

Bap! Bap! Bap! Bap! The drone spun wildly in a tight circle, then flipped on its side and accelerated toward the floor at a forty-five-degree angle, missing the truck by a couple of feet. Then it slid across the concrete and exploded against the warehouse's steel wall in a ball of red, orange, and yellow flames.

French and two men appeared from the hallway with chemical fire extinguishers. They extinguished the line of fire nearest the office area, and then moved to the stacked boxes. When both fires were extinguished, they emptied their remaining foam onto the burning wreckage of the drone.

French found the remains of the camera that had been attached to the drone. He looked into its lens, and screamed, "Estas muerto! Estas muerto aunque lo sepa o no!"

"What did you say to him?" I asked.

French dropped the camera onto the concrete floor. He had a wild look in his eyes, perhaps fear as much as anger. "I told the drone operator he was a dead man, whether he knows it or not."

French shouted orders at his men. They immediately began pulling apart the stack of boxes, separating them and ensuring the fire had been completely extinguished.

"We're all lucky," French said to me. "Those boxes contain hand grenades, but none of them exploded."

"Where the heck did you get hand grenades?"

He didn't look at me but watched as his men worked to clean up the mess which earlier had been a clean warehouse floor. "Military surplus, Fort Drum."

"No shit?"

"No shit. They cost me eight of the balloons Juanita and Rosalba brought into the country."

"And you traded them to somebody at Fort Drum? I never would have guessed."

"Military pay sucks, so enterprising young men find ways to earn extra money."

"By selling hand grenades?"

"Sometimes I buy bazookas."

Chapter Twenty-Four

Before I left Cabrillo Construction on the day of the drone attack, I had asked Caesar for a special favor, hinting it might help me solve the case of his two murdered men, Perez and Herrera.

"What do you need, my friend?" he had asked.

"You told me one of your men has a girlfriend who warned him about a possible assault by Onondaga. I'd like to talk with her. I'll be friendly."

"Do you think she knew of the drone attack but didn't warn us?"

"No. I think they planned an attack but called it off after you bombed their building."

Caesar smiled.

"The drone attack was something new," I said. "Maybe only one or two men planned it. Certainly, we hadn't planned a defense for it. I think they wanted to see if it would work. I think it did work to a degree, but they didn't have a good target in mind, or things would have been a whole lot worse."

French nodded. His eyes were focused on something in his mind. Something he didn't share with me. He would not commit to setting up a meeting. "I'll see what I can do. I don't want to set the young woman up for any trouble with her brother."

On Saturday, French called. "Rosalita Vieques is willing to meet with you after noon mass tomorrow. Her brother works at Onondaga as part of Los Cuernos' small army. I want to remind you they're vicious when it comes to informers."

I was due at Cabrillo Construction at two. So, at one o'clock I stopped for lunch at Ruby's Red Hots, then found my way across town to the Cabrillo warehouses.

I stopped at the checkpoint a few minutes before two and then drove to Warehouse Four where Rosalita and French were to be waiting for me in an unmarked white limousine.

I drove inside the open warehouse door and parked beside a white Cadillac stretch limo whose rear window had been painted with the words JUST MARRIED. I exited my Bronco. The limo's side door opened. I climbed in and shut the door behind me.

The woman across from me was dressed in a wedding gown with a long veil covering her face. If I had known her, I would never have been able to recognize her on the street, and I think that was the idea.

French made introductions and then encouraged me to begin with my questions.

"Thank you for your willingness to meet with me today. I know this meeting puts you at great risk, and I will do nothing to compromise your position."

She turned her head toward Caesar, who said something soothing to her in Spanish. She turned back to me and nodded.

"I want to know the name of the snake at Onondaga Trash."

She shrugged her shoulders. She had no idea what I was asking for.

"Somebody at Onondaga is a snake in human form. Can you guess who that might be?"

Caesar looked at me like I was out of my mind. "You asked me to set up this meeting so you can claim an animal has taken human form? Have you been taking drugs?"

"I'm sorry," I replied. "I know it sounds crazy, but somebody at Onondaga is a snake, or has a snake's name, or is called 'the snake.' I need his name. He knows what happened to Perez and Herrera."

French said something to Rosalita in Spanish. She spoke back in a low voice, as if I might understand what she was saying if she spoke in a louder voice. I have made that same mistake before, but in reverse, when speaking with people with limited English language ability. Several times I have found myself shouting at them, as though by forcing my words into their ears, they would be able to comprehend. As Bugs Bunny used to say, "What a maroon."

My mind was drifting when French brought me back to reality. "Rosalita thinks you may be seeking a man they call 'El Serpiente.' "

"The serpent?" I asked.

"Si," Rosalita said. "El Serpiente is the name my brother has said aloud several times when he has complained about things he must do at work. El Serpiente is the...how you say...the big boss...of Los Cuernos."

"Do you mean of the national organization?" I asked.

"No," she replied. "Local leader, but still top boss, big man, perro superior."

I looked at French.

"Top dog."

"Oh."

"Rosalita means El Serpiente is the head of the Los Cuernos group working at Onondaga," French explained. "He's not the big regional leader of the cartel, but he's been given command of the locals. I would call him a captain, but not a colonel. He still holds the keys to a man's life."

"Do you know his name?" I asked French.

He said something to Rosalita. She replied, "Señor Dario Estrada."

French looked at me. "Dario…"

"Estrada," I said.

"Si. Do you know him?"

I shook my head. "No. Do you?"

"I have met him one time…at a festival in Little Havana. He oozes confidence. I did not know he was Los Cuernos. But from his demeanor I should have suspected."

"Does it make a difference?"

"When you know a dog is vicious and might bite you, do you treat him differently than if you have no fear of him?"

I didn't respond, but already I could see the wheels turning in Caesar's head. Perez and Muñoz both had been decapitated, perhaps while still alive. Such an execution could easily be attributed to Los Cuernos, since decapitation by machete has been the organization's hallmark since its earliest beginnings in San Antonio, Texas.

I thanked Rosalita, exited the limo, and drove to Mariaville to ponder my next move.

****

When I got home, Joey Astor was standing in the driveway talking with a man in tan slacks and a denim jacket. His sandy orange hair complemented the orange lenses of his sunglasses.

"You're going to have to relocate for about two months," Joey told me. "This here is Warren Sawyer. He's the contractor who will be restoring the property."

I shook Sawyer's hand. "So, you're not building new?"

"I'd like to," Joey replied, "but the insurance company shorted me a little due to the condition of the structure prior to the damage."

"How much more do you need to build new?" I asked.

He waved a set of drawings in front of me. "Warren and I had planned to build this baby, but I'm about ten thousand short of what I need to do that. So, we're going to rebuild what we have."

"Let me see the drawings," I replied.

Warren Sawyer dropped the tailgate of his pickup truck. Joey laid the drawings out and pressed them flat with his palms. The cover displayed a beautiful two-story lake house with an above ground deck and floor to ceiling glass facing the setting sun.

Joey and Warren explained all the details to me, and I nodded as they did.

"Listen," I asked. "Is there any chance you could add a detached two-car garage with an apartment above it? You know, something you might rent to a private investigator?"

Joey smirked. "Do you know a good one?"

"How much extra would the garage cost?" I asked.

"Something to look appropriate for this house would cost around seventeen thousand," Sawyer said. "Appliances and furnishing for the apartment would be extra,"

"I'll give you a bank check for seventeen thousand dollars tomorrow, Joey. I'll also find your extra ten thousand before your home construction is completed. I'll pay you in cash."

"You're kidding me…"

"No, I'm serious. You helped me out when I needed it the most. This will be my way of repaying you. There is a catch, however."

"Here it comes," Joey said rolling his eyes at Sawyer.

"I want a legal document…a lease for the apartment that gives me the right to live in it rent free until twenty-five thousand dollars in rent equivalent has been reached."

Sawyer looked at Joey. "Grab it, pal. If you rent the apartment for eight hundred dollars a month, that's only two and a half years. Then you can kick the rent up to a thousand a month and kick out the freeloader."

We all laughed.

Joey thought about it for a few moments and then stuck out his hand. "It's a deal. But if you don't come up with the extra ten grand by the end of construction, I'm going to have a take on a mortgage, so all bets would be off. I'll need to rent the apartment to make the mortgage payments."

I reached out and shook his hand. "I'll call you tomorrow and set a time to meet so I can give you the check.

Sawyer rolled up the blueprints. "Looks like I'll have to get these blueprints on the agenda of the Mariaville Town Building Committee so we can get them approved," he said enthusiastically. "I could have your new lake home completed by the end of July."

"One last request," I said. "Any chance you could build the garage before you build the house? I don't seem to have a place to live."

"If it's okay with Joey. It'll give me a good place to store materials. I could keep everything on the floor of the garage to keep it out of the rain."

Joey nodded. "Do it."

"Thanks, Joey. I think we're both winners on this deal."

"Yeah, I think you're right. And my wife is going to do backflips when I tell her."

Chapter Twenty-Five

"Hi, Helen, it's me. I've got a favor to ask."

"You always wanting something, Jonesy, but you never wanting me." She paused a second and exhaled into the receiver. "What is it this time?"

"Can you run a name through your new computing system and see what you discover about this bad boy? I need an address, too."

"Sure, Jonesy. What's the name?"

"Dario Estrada. He probably lives in the Capital Region."

"What you working on now?"

I was working on Perez and Herrera, but Helen didn't know about Herrera. "Same case as you—Perez and Muñoz. You got any new leads?"

"I just closed the file 'cause there's been nothing new in quite a while. Everything has led to a dead end."

"Call me when you get the info, okay?"

"Well, I sure can't walk it up to your desk."

Helen called me half an hour later. "Your guy Estrada was in a few scrapes in the Bronx a couple of years back. He's never done any time. Some indication he might have ties to the Los Cuernos gang, but nothing absolute. Got a pencil?"

"Yeah."

"He lives at an Albany address, but it's on the fringe of Colonie. Nice neighborhood...number fifteen

LaGrange. I checked it out on Google/maps. Four-bedroom executive ranch with a three-car garage and a pool out back. You need me to contact Colonie Police to get permission to investigate him?"

"No permission needed for a private dick, Helen. You want to come sit in the car with me? I'm going on stakeout."

"Are you asking me out on a date? There's lots of nice restaurants in Colonie."

"The best I can offer is coffee and donuts, unless you opt for a bagel with cream cheese."

"You do the first day. If nothing happens, I might join you on the second day. Maybe we can catch up while we discuss why some immigrant with no visible means of support lives in a house we can't afford."

****

Helen was right about the neighborhood. LaGrange was the last street in northwest Albany. As I drove into the neighborhood, I felt humbled by its opulence. Its homes were large and well-kept, and the streets were well-paved and quiet. Its back yards butted up against similarly nice homes in Colonie, a suburb full of white-collar workers who commuted daily to state government jobs in Albany. Most of their kids came home on clean school buses or drove themselves home in hand-me-down BMWs or Mercedes to single family estates with manicured lawns. This was a neighborhood insulated from the poverty which was rampant in the City of Albany and nearby Troy.

When I found number fifteen LaGrange, I realized a normal stakeout would be impossible because nobody parked on the street in that neighborhood. My best bet would be to observe from afar, perhaps by video camera, but I lacked the resources and technological know-how to set that up. I opted for a basic trail cam which I purchased for under a hundred dollars and strapped to a pine tree on a neighbor's property directly across from Estrada's driveway. After two days, and dressed as a tree pruner, I retrieved the memory card from the camera and replaced it and the camera's eight AA batteries with new ones.

Demolition of my temporary home in Mariaville had not yet begun, so I continued to use it as my primary residence. I returned home with the memory card and inserted it into my laptop. The card had stored over four hundred pictures, so I thought examining them closely would take several hours. I was wrong. Many of the pictures were of cars, trucks, and school busses passing by on the street. Dog walkers, bicyclists, and joggers ate a lot of space, too. Then, a bunch of kids were playing out front. They amassed a third of the pictures. However, I got a handful of nice pics of a vehicle which did not belong in the neighborhood—an old El Camino that was badly in need of repair. I figured it belonged to either a gardener or an illegal. I decided to have its plate run.

Helen didn't answer when I called, so I left her a message, "Helen, it's Bart. Can you run a plate for me?" I left her the number and asked her to call me when she had something.

She called me an hour later. "Sorry I couldn't call sooner. I was in a meeting with the chief. We've got too many unsolved murders. He threatened to fire all of us and hire back the cops who could really get it done. You were one of the ones he mentioned."

Her comment made me smile, but I didn't think I would go back, even if the chief begged. My current gig was just too good, and the freedom to work without the restrictions of department policies or someone looking over my shoulder was too good to give up.

"Did you get my message about the license plate?"

"Yeah. The El Camino is registered to Ramon Robles. He lives outside of Albany, near Voorheesville. I've already emailed his rural route box number to you." She paused a second. "I thought you were going to take me on your stakeout. You didn't even call."

"I had to set up a trail cam because there was no place to park inconspicuously. When you see the place, you'll understand."

"You need help talking with Robles? I need a break on this case because, like I said, the chief is threatening to fire all of us if we don't solve a few cases."

"Yeah. Assuming Robles has some kind of job, I thought I would drop in on him at dinner time. Want to ride with me or meet me there?"

"Let's ride together. I'll meet you at the Walmart parking lot at five thirty. I'll be parked near the old one-day photo booth."

"Great, Helen. Come in plain clothes."

"I'm not dressing up in a uniform for this guy. I'll bet he doesn't even speak English."

****

Ramon Robles was arranging bags of black mulch in the back of his El Camino when Helen and I pulled into his driveway. Standing sideways to us, he looked up at Helen's Hyundai in surprise. He was a short man with an oily crop of black hair and a gut that protruded four burritos out from his belt line. He was dressed in a drab white sleeveless tee shirt, green work pants, and steel toed ankle boots. I had seen his kind before, usually working at golf courses and at the county's recycling center. They are hard workers, minimal complainers, and often—but not always—illegals.

When we climbed out of my Bronco, Helen was the first to speak.

"Mr. Robles?"

"Si," he replied, wiping his hands on a red oil rag.

"I'm Detective Helen Martin, Willow Falls Police Department. I need your help in solving two missing persons investigations."

"Who's the hombre with you?"

"This is Bart Jones. He's assisting in my investigation."

"You don' look like no police officer."

"I'm a detective," Helen replied. "Sometimes we work in plainclothes."

Robles threw the red rag into the back of his El Camino. "I don' know no missing hombres."

"An anonymous caller told me you might know the whereabouts of a gentleman named Muñoz."

"I read in the newspaper that hombre was found dead. Have you checked the graveyard?"

"How about a guy named Jorge Perez? Do you know him or his whereabouts?"

"Same thing, lady. I read he was dead, too. He was killed by a bear."

As I expected, Helen was getting nowhere. Machos don't care for successful women—or nosy women for that matter—and Helen smacked of both success and nosiness.

"Do you know anybody who might know anything about the disappearance of those two men?" she asked.

"Nope."

"Do you know where these men worked or where they hung out when they weren't working?"

"I don' know nothing about those hombres," Robles repeated. "I never saw them before."

"Before when?"

"Come on, Helen. This guy is a dead end," I said.

Robles shot me an angry look. Maybe he thought I had insulted him in some way.

Helen handed him a business card. "Well, if you can think of anything which might help me in my investigation, please give me a call."

I escorted Helen back to her car and then got in while she was snapping her seatbelt.

"I don't know why I thought Robles could be helpful," she said. "He's offering nothing, but I'm sure he knows plenty."

Helen drove me back to Walmart to get my car.

"You want some dinner?" she asked.

"Yes, but just something quick. Would you do a burger if I bought?"

I hopped out of her car, and into mine. Helen followed me to Topsy's diner. We ordered dinner and then carried our bags to an empty booth.

"You're kind of quiet, Jonesy."

"Yeah. I've thought up a plan, but I need your help to pull it off."

Helen rolled her eyes. "One of those, huh? You'd better tell me about it."

I didn't beat around the bush. "Can you borrow a cadaver from the morgue?"

Helen pressed backwards into the orange cushion of her booth. "You're kidding me. That's got to be some kind of state or federal crime."

"I just want to borrow one…maybe a homeless person. I'm thinking I might be able to get Robles to expose his complicity in the Herrera and Perez murders."

"How am I going to be able to get you a cadaver?"

"You're resourceful. You'll think of a way. Just call me when you have it."

Helen dropped her burger onto its paper plate. "Have it where? At home? Hell, no."

"When you have it on a gurney at the department. Maybe I can meet you at the motor pool when the shift changes, at the dock where the ambulances drop off cadavers."

"I'm not so sure I want in on this. I could lose my job."

"If you don't solve those two murders, you might be back on a beat, anyway."

Helen sat quietly for a moment. "Okay," she nodded. "You've done some crazy stuff before, but it's always helped solve cases. If I can manage to get my hands on a cadaver, I'll call you."

I think she was trying to convince herself I wouldn't do something which would get her into trouble.

"But you'd better not dillydally around when I call."

I nodded. "Yes, ma'am." I pointed at the red spot on her white pullover top. "You wear that ketchup very well."

Chapter Twenty-Six

Two days later, Helen called me. "Shift changes at four thirty. You be waiting for me at the motor pool at four thirty-five. Back up to the loading dock. I got the cadaver you want. Just came in this morning. Homeless white guy. Been stabbed three times."

"Did the M.E. already examine the body?"

"He's on vacation for the next three days, and the body is in the cooler waiting for him to return."

"So, my loaner has to be back in three days."

"That's about the size of it, Jonesy."

Hey, I couldn't complain. Helen had actually found me a cadaver. It was at that point I realized she would do just about anything for me. I could never say that about Rachel, my ex-wife.

****

I was at the motor pool at four twenty-eight, backed up to the loading dock with my motor running.

The shift supervisor walked up to me, carrying a clipboard in his right hand. "What are you picking up?"

"Non-identified load of crap from homicide. I'm taking it to Albany FBI office for analysis. It may not be on your list. You know how the Feds are."

"Yeah. Just let Findley know what you're doing. He should be here by five after."

Findley would be the second shift supervisor. "Okay, will do."

The shift supervisor walked back into his shed and probably out through its interior door.

After his shed door closed, I heard a slamming metallic sound and saw Helen walking straight toward me, pushing a sheet-covered gurney.

"Got your commodity," she said. "Help me get it off this thing, would you?"

The back gate of my Bronco was down, and its rear window was up in loading position. I grabbed the covered corpse, only to realize I had the foot end rather than the head.

"Spin the gurney around, would you?"

"Take him like he is," Helen replied. "I don't have time for any gymnastics."

I shrugged my shoulders and pulled the corpse off the gurney while backing myself into the Bronco. The body dropped with a "thud." I thought the head might fall off, but it didn't. But the sheet caught on the edge of the gurney and the body was completely exposed in the back end of my Bronco. Somebody was coming, so I quickly tugged at the sheet while Helen tried to pry it free from the edge of the gurney. The gurney fell over with a loud clatter, but the sheet dislodged, and I was able to cover the body quickly.

"Get out of here with that thing, Jonesy," Helen urged. "And call me when you've done what you're going to do so we can schedule getting Spooky here back into the cooler."

I blew her a kiss, closed the back end of my Bronco, and drove out of the motor pool.

I got home at five thirty and backed into my parking area so when my rear hatch was open, nobody driving by would see what I was doing.

Because he was waiting for the medical examiner, Spooky was naked. I rummaged through my closet and found some older clothes I didn't wear too often and decided to give them to the homeless.

Dressing a cadaver gave me renewed respect for morticians because Spooky did not cooperate with the process. He was a little stiff—no pun intended—so getting his arms into my old blue and yellow plaid shirt was difficult. I had to hold him up with my hip, and after slipping his right arm into its sleeve, I had to pry his left arm backward until its elbow bent just enough to maneuver the sleeve onto it. When I was finished, I wished I had lifted both arms above his head and slid both sleeves on at the same time. It might have been an easier job.

Putting my old pale blue slacks onto him was easier because, although they were bent at the knees, his legs were essentially parallel. I hated to give away my black belt, but I only wore it to funerals and weddings. As I was slipping it through the loops on the slacks, I mused that in many cases, like mine, a wedding was often the commencement of a process of slow death for both parties in the ritual. So, why do we make such a big celebration out of it? I would have to think about that for a while.

I also gave away a pair of my black socks and the black lace-up shoes I used to wear when I was in my dress blues as a cop. Then I carried my battery-powered electric razor out to the Bronco and gave Spooky a quick shave. I left the hair on his head alone.

When I was finished, Spooky didn't look too bad. He had been dead for a day, and now he looked better than when he had found his way to the morgue. So, I shut the Bronco's rear hatch and drove to Voorheesville, where I found Ramon Robles' home.

When I pulled into Robles' driveway, the sun was setting over the Helderbergs, a mountainous escarpment a few miles west of town. A flatbed truck was parked beside his El Camino, its orange cab almost the same color as the sky. The sound of my tires on the gravel driveway drew Robles and another man out of his home.

I climbed out of my Bronco. "Ola, Señor Robles."

"Have we met before?"

The man with Robles moved three paces to my left. He must have been unsure if I was going to cause trouble.

"Yes, I came here several days ago with that woman police detective."

"Yeah, I 'member you now. Wha' you want?"

"I need your help." I held both palms up, like a beggar in Old Town Tijuana. "Although I came here with that policewoman, I'm not a police officer and it has nothing to do with the police."

"Wha' you need?"

"I'm hoping you can help me with a disposal problem. I've heard you have done that for people before."

"Who would say something like that? I don' know what you talking 'bout."

"Señor, I have done much work for the Mexican Banditos and other gangs. Just a few weeks ago I helped smuggle two women from Sinaloa into this country. I picked them up in Canada and brought them across the St. Lawrence River."

"Wha' you want…a medal?"

"I want to hire you to help me with a problem. Your services are renown."

"Two putas, huh?" He spit a hocker onto the ground. "Wha's you problem?"

I pointed toward the other man. "Is this gentleman trustworthy?"

"Si, hombre. All us Mexicanos know how to silence our tongues." His directness surprised me. It was a sign of greater intelligence than I had estimated.

I motioned for Robles to follow me to the back of my Bronco. His friend followed right along. I dropped the back gate and lifted the rear window. "This is my problem."

When Robles and his friend looked in the cargo area, I pulled the sheet off Spooky.

"You *do* got a problem, gringo. Who killed this hombre?"

"That's my business. What I need is your expert assistance in disposing of the body. Are you interested?"

"It's gonna cost you," Robles said, looking at his friend. "Wha' you think, Pasquale?"

The other man nodded. "Si, it's gonna cost you, gringo."

"How much?"

"Two thousand," Robles said.

"Ouch, I don't have two thousand. Would you take one thousand? You don't have to kill him. That's already been taken care of. He can't fight back. He can't cut you."

"You gotta find more money, gringo. Once we take this body off your hands, we taking all the risk."

"How about twelve hundred?"

Pasquale jumped in. "Thirteen hundred is the least we'll take."

"Excuse us, gringo," Robles said. "Me and

Pasquale, we gotta talk."

The two men walked around the side of Robles house. I could hear Robles giving Pasquale "what for." I jumped at the opportunity to pull a small magnetic device from my pocket and attach it behind the El Camino's rear bumper. Then I returned to the back end of my Bronco.

When the arguing beside the house simmered down, the two men reappeared. Pasquale was the first to speak. "I'm sorry, gringo. The very least we can take is fifteen hundred dollars."

"But you said thirteen hundred."

"He forgot we have to buy gasoline for the El Camino," Robles said. "It drinks a lot of gas."

I pretended to give it much thought, then I nodded. "Okay. If you'll do it for fifteen hundred, then we have a bargain."

"In cash, up front," Robles said.

I opened my wallet. I had fourteen hundred dollars in cash, so I pulled it out and counted it into Robles' eagerly waiting hand.

"Tha's only fourteen, gringo," Robles said.

"I've got some twenties in my glove compartment."

We walked to the passenger side of my Bronco. I opened the door, leaned in, and let Robles watch over my shoulder as I pulled a white envelope from beneath my forty-five semi-automatic pistol. I opened the envelope and removed five twenties. They were all confiscated counterfeits, but they were high quality and Robles would not know they were bad unless he tried to deposit them at the bank.

"Keep your hands off your pistola, gringo," Robles warned.

"If I were going to rob you, I wouldn't be giving you my own money, Señor Robles. Besides, we're conducting business. I left my pistol in the glove compartment so you would see I am an honest man and I mean you no harm."

"Si, gringo. Entiendo."

Robles and his friend Pasquale wrestled Spooky out of my Bronco and dropped him into the bed of the El Camino.

"You need that sheet?" Robles asked.

"It's all yours."

He smiled, picked it off the ground, and handed it to Pasquale. Pasquale fluffed it over Spooky like he was making a bed, and then he began putting forty-pound bags of mulch on top of the cadaver.

"Don' you worry none, gringo. Pasquale and me, we'll dispose of your friend before midnight in a place where nobody will ever find him."

"Thank you, Señor. It's been nice doing business with you."

"Si. Same here."

I climbed into my empty Bronco, started its engine, and backed out of the driveway. I turned toward Albany. A mile down the road, I pulled into a Stewart's Shoppe and waited for my portable GPS system to indicate Robles and his friend Pasquale were on the road with Spooky. Ten minutes later, when the system detected motion, I started my motor and headed back toward Robles' home. Robles and Pasquale had turned right out of his driveway and were headed toward Mariaville. I was pretty certain I knew where they were going, but I needed to be sure, and I could not let them get more than five miles away from me or the GPS system would lose track of their position.

As I suspected, Ramon Robles and his friend Pasquale were not too bright. They opted for expedience over intelligence and stopped on the ridge behind Naomi Malbrook's. When they stopped, I shut my headlights and coasted to within a half mile of them. I sat on the shoulder of the road until the red dot on the GPS screen showed them heading back toward me. Headlights still off, I quickly pulled onto the gravel road which led to Naomi's camp and coasted to a stop so my brake lights would not give me away. Less than a minute later, headlights passed by on the hard surface road behind me. From the outline of the vehicle against the darkening sky, I could tell it was an El Camino. They already had done their work and were headed home.

I called Helen.

"Well…?" she asked without saying "hello."

"I think we've got them. I won't know until morning, but I think Robles and a friend of his dumped the homeless guy on the hillside above Naomi Malbrook's home on Mariaville Lake."

"Really?"

"Yeah. Same location as the other two cadavers. Those two hombres are going to be our link to whoever killed Herrera and Perez."

Chapter Twenty-Seven

I woke up at seven but didn't leave my cabin until eight o'clock in the morning, when most of the hourly workers were on the job and the road traffic on the hill behind Naomi Malbrook's home would be light. I stopped at the Mariaville store and bought two donuts and a black coffee to go. Then I drove up the hill behind Naomi's and slowly crept along until I saw a spot where the eighteen-inch-tall grass on the shoulder had recently been pressed down by tires. Without doubt, Robles and his sidekick Pasquale had stopped here to earn their quick fifteen hundred dollars.

I passed by the tire marks, so I wouldn't disturb them, and parked my Bronco on the side of the road with its flashers blinking. I walked along the hillside on the safe side of the guardrail, watching my footing because I didn't want to slide downhill unexpectedly. Sure enough, a tangled body lay at the bottom of the hill parallel to the spot where the grass had been pressed down by Robles' El Camino. Even from thirty feet above, I could see my blue and yellow checked shirt through the thistles and raspberry vines.

I called Helen, reported what I had found, and she did the rest from her office. At nine thirty, a state police cruiser pulled up behind my Bronco.

A tall officer got out and walked up to me, resting the palm of his right hand on the grips of his revolver.

"You found a body?"

I pointed over the guardrail. "Yessir, right down there."

He stepped forward and looked. "How'd you ever see it way down there?"

I held up my empty coffee cup. "I stopped to pee and there it was. I reported it to a friend of mine who's with the Willow Falls Police Department. I knew she'd know who to contact."

The officer nodded. He asked for my name and contact information. "You can get on with your business now. If we have more questions for you, we'll be in touch."

I took that to mean he wanted me out of the way before a crew arrived to extricate the body from the thorn bushes. That was fine by me. I shook his hand and drove back down the hill to Naomi's driveway. I felt like my job was done for the day, and I could take a brief hiatus by helping Naomi with her weed pulling for a couple of hours before I connected with Helen to see what she had done about Robles and Pasquale. I was wrong.

I pulled into Naomi's driveway and parked beside her green Subaru station wagon. I expected to see her out and about, but she wasn't in the water pulling weeds and I didn't see her standing in her garden. I got out of my Bronco and knocked on her door. "Naomi?" I called out.

Old Jake ran from a rose bush beside her house and took refuge under a lilac bush in her side yard. I knocked on the door again. "Naomi?"

There was no response, so fearing the worst, I walked into her home and checked all the rooms. She was not inside. I thought she probably was next door, visiting the Faulkners, so I stepped back outside and cut through her garden to knock on the door of the Faulkner's cabin. As I passed through a tall row of Brussels sprouts, I saw Naomi lying face down, her head twisted sideways and her tongue hanging out. Two flies were taking turns landing near her eyes on her ashen face. I had seen her expression before on a dead deer, shot by my friend David when we were in high school hunting big game for the first time. I held no hope Naomi was alive.

I bent down and held my sunglasses under Naomi's nostrils. No breath collected on the lenses. I rolled her onto her back and began pounding on her ribs with my fist, hoping to jar her heart back into action. Then I began CPR, as we had been taught at the department, pushing on her chest to the beat of "Another One Bites the Dust."

"Faulkner," I yelled. "Faulkner, help."

Anna Faulkner came to the screen door. "How can I help you?"

"Call 9-1-1 and tell them we have a woman down, possible heart attack. It's Naomi Malbrook."

"Oh dear." Anna disappeared into her cabin.

Emma popped her head out the screen door. I heard Anna yell at her. "No, stay inside, Emma."

Emma shut the screen door and did as her mom had ordered. Suddenly the door popped back open, and Marv Faulkner hurried across the yard to see if he could lend assistance.

"Is she alive?"

"I don't think so, Marv. I'm trying CPR but she doesn't seem to be responding."

"What do you think has happened?"

"Heart attack or stroke. I'm no doctor, so I don't really know."

"Anna's called the rescue squad. They'll be here in short order."

I pushed down again and again on Naomi's chest. Marv wiped dirt out of her mouth and off her face. Soon we could hear sirens and shortly afterward the sound of truck tires on the gravel driveway.

The paramedics arrived and approached us quickly. The larger one looked at Naomi and shook his head. "She ain't lookin' too good, is she?"

The shorter paramedic covered Naomi's nose and mouth with the mask of a battery-operated breathing apparatus. Then the larger paramedic opened a defibrillator. He tore open Naomi's blouse and placed the sticky paddles on the wrinkled skin of her chest. "Ya'll stand back or you might get shocked."

We did as he instructed.

The paramedic hit a button on the defibrillator and Naomi's chest heaved. He shocked her a second time and then listened to her heart. He shocked her a third time and a fourth. He listened to her heart again. "Ain't no use. She's a goner."

Marv and I stood silent as the paramedics brought a stretcher over to the garden, strapped Naomi on it, and carried her to their ambulance. Once the ambulance departed, Anna and Emma walked out of their cabin and joined Marv and me in the garden.

"Looks like she was picking Brussels sprouts," Anna said.

"You may as well help yourself to everything she has in her garden," I replied. "I know she'd want you to enjoy it."

"I suppose." Anna turned to her daughter. "Emma, would you go get a colander from under the kitchen counter. There are two of them near the mixing bowls."

Emma ran off to do her mother's bidding.

"I'm glad Emma didn't find Naomi," Marv said. "I don't think she'd ever forget an experience like that."

Anna slowly shook her head. "And we were just beginning to appreciate our relationship with Naomi as a friend."

Marv pointed to the cat, who was now sitting on Naomi's deck. "Somebody is going to have to take Old Jake in and care for him. Looks like it might be us. I think Emma is the best friend he has right now."

I nodded.

"Would you care for some Brussels sprouts?" Anna asked.

I pulled a plant from the ground and shook its roots free of dirt. "There are enough on this stalk for two or three meals."

Anna plucked two yellow squashes from a low-lying plant. "Take these, too. It'll be Naomi's way of saying 'thanks' for everything you did to try to save her life."

"I just wish I had arrived sooner. I was delayed helping the state police retrieve another body from up above."

"Another dumping?" Marv asked.

"Yeah, only this time we know who did it, so it'll probably be the last time it ever happens."

"Good," Anna said. "Just the thought of that bear eating a dead human being gives me the willies."

"Amen," I replied.

Chapter Twenty-Eight

Roxanne Windsor had moved. I met her at her new place, a three-thousand square foot gray stone home in the historic Stockade section of Schenectady. The Stockade would have been only an older neighborhood in a depressed river town, except in sixteen-ninety its Dutch inhabitants were slaughtered by the French and Indians in a surprise attack. Thus, it had been denoted a possibly haunted "historic site."

Roxanne was waiting for me when I rang her doorbell. In fact, she opened the front door before her chimes stopped ringing.

"Good evening, Barty," she said.

Roxanne was dressed to the nines in the latest evening fashion—a blue floral print maxi dress and pink cowboy boots. She handed me a short white leather jacket. "In case it gets colder later."

She pulled her door closed and locked the deadbolt. Then we climbed into her Bentley for a quick ride to dinner. She drove.

"Where are we headed?" I asked.

"Libertine's. You ever been there?"

"It's that place in Esperance?"

"Nope. That's Lupertino's. Libertine's is in Charlton."

Charlton is an expensive rural suburb north of Willow Falls and Glenville. Many of its homes are gentlemen's farms with very long driveways and huge manicured yards which are mowed by large lawn tractors, most often driven by hired labor.

"I guess I've never been there," I replied.

"You're going to love it. The décor is farmhouse, but the wine list is extensive and there are no prices on the menu."

"No prices? How do they get away with that?"

"The food is better than they serve at Windsor Palace and the White House. If you can't afford to eat there, you should make reservations somewhere else."

I was carrying only one hundred fifty dollars, and my credit card was close to being maxed out. "I think I should have dumped some money on my credit card before we left. I had no idea we were going to such an expensive venue."

"It's going to be fine, Barty. I have a gift certificate for two, and it includes two drinks each. You'll just have to spring for any extras and the gratuity."

"You've thought of everything, Roxanne. So why did you decide to splurge on me instead of another eligible bachelor?"

Roxanne smiled and squeezed my thigh just above the kneecap, where the leg is extra sensitive. "There's just something 'je ne sais quois' about you, Barty, that sends Kundalini up my spine. You get my juices flowing. Besides, I like a man who can handle his gun."

She was being blunt about where our evening was headed. It was a promise which sent anticipation through my body. Roxanne was attractive and had a wild side I had discovered while investigating the death of seven-year-old Laura Moretti. It had been a while since I had been with a woman, and Roxanne seemed like a tiger who could not be tamed. Or, well, maybe she just tickled my leg in the right spot. Regardless, I felt the tingle of arousal and I looked forward to a romp in the hay if she was still willing after she watched me eat.

We ordered from the menu and, as Roxanne said, it offered no prices. But our dinners were freebies. We began with cocktails. Roxanne had a Bloody Mary and I had a Whistlepig on the rocks. When the waitress returned, she asked our orders.

"I'll have the house salad, vegetables of the day, and filet mignon, seared quickly for no more than thirty seconds each side," Roxanne said.

The waitress scrunched her face. "That's almost raw."

"Yes, and I eat most fruits and oysters the same way."

The waitress turned to me. "Do you want yours the same way?"

"No, actually I'm intrigued by the prawns Provencal with ratatouille."

"The prawns will be cooked."

"Yes, I hope so."

She smiled and then departed to give our orders to the chef. She returned quickly with a basket of assorted dinner rolls and a dish of thymed butter. Then she turned to chat with the guests at another table. They were probably paying customers. Maybe regulars.

Roxanne removed a bread stick from the basket. She put the end of it in her mouth and swirled her tongue around it seductively.

"How's your love life, Barty?" she asked. "Are you seeing anybody special?"

I hadn't dated anyone in months. I shook my head.

"You're as special as it gets, Roxanne."

She smiled. "Well, maybe we'll have to do this more often…get you out and noticed by the single ladies."

My life, at least the portion I could share, was basically boring. All the exciting stuff verged on illegal activities. So, I changed the subject.

"Tell me more about your chapter of the Black Hat Society. The information your ladies gave us was spot-on. Well, at least we think so. It gave us a good lead and we think we've identified the 'snake.' "

"The snake among the discarded of the people of the hills?"

"Yes. We just have to figure out how to capture him. Evidence is sparce and any witnesses are dead."

"Can you share who it is?"

"You know I can't divulge the details of an ongoing investigation. I wish I could. Maybe when the case has been solved by the police and the murderer has been tried for his crimes."

"My girls will be pleased to learn the results of our séance have been helpful. That's why we formed, you know…to help our community."

Our meals arrived. Roxanne's looked especially bloody, and I knew she ordered it for that reason. My prawns smelled scrumptious, and my first forkful was tasty.

"Anytime you want to bring me back here, I'll come without any reservations."

Roxanne smiled. "They won't seat you unless you've called ahead, Barty."

"You know what I mean, Roxanne."

She laughed. "Where do you live, Barty? I can only imagine a beefy place like a loft or a retro garage."

"I live in a piece of Swiss cheese."

"Come on, Barty. I'm being serious. I see you living in a place that's been converted from industrial use to contemporary living space."

"I'm being serious, too. I rent a place on a lake. But it looks like Swiss cheese because it was shot up by a truckload of men using automatic weapons. They put more than a hundred holes in the place. It's going to be renovated soon. Actually, it's going to be demolished and rebuilt. And I'll get to live over the garage when it's completed. So, you're partly right."

Her eyes opened wide. "Oh, shot up, like full of bullet holes?"

"Yeah, exactly like that. Over a hundred of them."

"And you weren't killed or wounded?"

"I'm living proof of my own continued existence."

"How marvelous. You're like 007…impervious. I like a man like that."

"Like what?"

"Impervious. You know, a man who can face down anything."

"I wouldn't say I'm really that kind of guy."

She ran her toes up my trousers leg. "Ooooh, eat up quickly, Barty. I want to take you home and check your body for scars and bullet holes."

We ordered a second round of drinks. She opted for a brandy, but I stuck with Whistlepig. Then we ordered desserts. I opted for flourless chocolate cake and Roxanne selected fruit trifle. "It's a traditional British favorite, and Libertine's knocks it out of the park," she said.

Five men weaved through the tables and placed instruments on a small bandstand that had been erected in the corner of the room. Their activity drew my attention to an oval dancefloor that I hadn't noticed earlier. Soon they were tuning up two guitars, a bass, a violin, and a mandolin.

Our desserts arrived. Before the waitress turned away, the band struck up a romantic number that I had heard before, but I couldn't name. "Care to dance?" I asked Roxanne.

Roxanne offered her hand, and I held it as she rose from her chair. I held my left out for her, but she threw her arms around my neck and hugged me closely as we danced. I was a bit awkward, but she followed every step and misstep as though we were one in thought and motion.

We hadn't finished dessert, but the waitress brought our bill. It was over five hundred dollars. Roxanne put the gift certificate in the guest cheque pad. The waitress picked it up and returned a few minutes later.

"The manager says you owe one hundred two dollars more."

"Our gift certificates covered dinner and two drinks," I explained. "Why the extra charge?"

"It's the Whistlepig," she explained. "You can have two free drinks, but not from the reserve offerings. Management gave you one, but you'll have to pay for the second."

"One hundred dollars per shot?" I asked.

"Oh, yes. They should have charged you more, but when they saw how you were dressed, they figured you couldn't afford it."

"Nice. You insult a guest and expect him to come back sometime?"

"Mister, I don't care if you come back or not.

Management says you owe another hundred two dollars."

I put my entire bankroll of one hundred fifty dollars in the cheque pad. The waitress was going to get a tip of forty-eight dollars, which was more than enough from my point of view. She probably thought I stiffed her.

"Come on, Barty," Roxanne said. "We're making a scene. Besides, I want to see your scars."

We left Libertine's. Roxanne drove us back to her house and parked beside my Bronco.

"How about a nightcap?" she asked.

I took that to mean she was still interested in a romp. I followed her into her home. She locked the door and then poured us two brandies. I had tasted better, but it was still good.

She put on some mood music and sat beside me on her sofa. It was a luxurious soft white suede. In less than five minutes we were making out. In less than ten, we were both naked. She straddled me and rode me like a stallion for another half hour. When I could not stand it anymore, I erupted. She screamed at the same moment. I guess she had been waiting for me. From my perspective, it was definitely worth the wait.

We lay beside each other on her sofa for twenty minutes and then she started kissing me again. That led to more screaming and erupting.

When I said goodnight, I promised I would call her and schedule another romp. Why not? She was unquestionably the tiger I thought she might be.

Chapter Twenty-Nine

It took Helen almost a full day to get verified identification on Robles' friend Pasquale. His real name was Santiago Ignacio Diaz. She was stymied by the name Pasquale, especially since it was not even vaguely associated with his real name. Albany County Social Services listed him as an "undocumented Mexican, awaiting a political asylum hearing." His hearing date had not yet been established, although he had lived in Albany County for more than two years.

She obtained consent for arrest and then waited until two patrol cars returned to the police station and the two men they had transported had been fingerprinted, photographed, and fully processed.

Finally, she received word they were both in holding cells. "Move Diaz into an interrogation room," she told the bailiff. Ten minutes later she received word Diaz was waiting for her in Interrogation Room Three.

Helen called Interrogation Support. "I need a Spanish translator in Interrogation Room Three."

"When you need the hombre?"

"Five minutes."

"Okay. You say 'Room Three,' right?"

Helen wanted to scream. The department had hired a cast of poorly prepared support people, mostly because of hiring quotas established by the city council. She hoped her translator was at least marginally fluent in

English and had been schooled on police protocols. That was not always the case. Most were learning on the job and their mistakes had caused the department a few mistrials.

"Yeah. See you in five minutes."

She took the elevator to the basement and followed the hallway to Interrogation Room Three. A lone guard was standing outside the door. She signaled to him to let her in. He inserted a key and pushed against the green steel door with his shoulder.

Diaz was sitting at a rectangular steel table. Its legs were bolted to the concrete floor. Diaz's legs and wrists were cuffed. In the light from the single bulb above him, Diaz looked miserable. He hadn't shaved in several days and his graying hair was dirty and unkempt.

Helen sat across the table from him. Diaz just stared at her, but it was not a menacing glare. She suspected he may have been confused by what was happening to him.

The door to the room opened. A thin man with a pointed goatee entered and sat beside Helen. "My name is Manuel Baez. I am your interpreter."

They shook hands and then Helen began the inquiry.

"Do you understand English?"

Diaz nodded.

"Good." She turned to Baez. "This may go well. Be sure he understands everything I say to him."

"Yes, ma'am."

She turned back to Diaz. "Your name is Santiago Ignacio Diaz. Correct?"

"Si, Señorita."

"So, why do they call you Pasquale?"

"When she was a baby, my mother came to Mexico from Italy. She gave birth to me on Easter morning. The name 'pascual,' means something to do with Easter. My family called me 'Little Pascual' until I was big enough to beat up anybody who called me names."

"You mean anyone who called you 'Pasquale'?"

"No. Anyone who called me 'Tonto' or 'Gordo.' "

Helen turned to Baez.

Baez smiled. "Anybody who called him 'stupid' or 'fat.' "

Helen nodded. She turned back to Diaz. "Do you know why you're here?"

Diaz thought for a moment. "No, Señorita."

"You've been charged with murder and the illegal disposal of human remains."

"I don' kill nobody."

Helen opened a folder and pulled out a photograph of the remains of Jorge Perez. "Do you know who this is?"

Diaz looked briefly at the picture. "How do I know who that hombre is? He doesn't got no head."

"This is the bear-eaten body of Jorge Perez. Does his name mean anything to you?"

"That hombre was bear food?"

"Yes. A bear found his body in a snowbank and fed on it for several days. Does his name mean anything to you?"

"What's his name again?"

"Jorge Perez."

"Never heard of him."

Helen pulled out a photograph of Perez's head. "This is Perez's face. His head was found on the highway, across the street from the location of the body. It's decomposed, but does he look familiar to you?"

"Mother of Mercy, Señorita. You showing me some

gross stuff."

Helen kept at him. She tapped her finger three times on the photo. "Do you recognize his face?"

"No, no, no. I don't know that hombre."

"His head was severed by a machete, the same type as we found in your friend's truck."

"In Ramon's truck?"

"Yes, under his front seat. It had dried blood on it. That blood is being analyzed by our labs, and if we find Perez's blood on it, the two of you will be in prison in no time."

"He uses the machete to chop bunches of bushes and tree limbs."

"It's also being analyzed for fingerprints. Will yours be on it?"

"Señorita, I used the machete to cut firewood just the other day."

Helen pulled another photo out of her folder. It was the homeless guy, still dressed the way he was found on the hill above Mrs. Malbrook's home. "Do you know this man?"

"Maybe I seen him somewhere. Can't be sure."

"You and Ramon Robles dumped his body on a hillside near Mariaville Lake."

"We don' kill nobody."

"We know you didn't kill this man. However, we have a witness who gave you the body and money to dispose of it."

"He didn't give me no money."

"He gave the money to Robles, and you and Ramon drove the body to Mariaville."

"That hombre say that about me?"

"Yes. He is a private detective, and he set you up.

You're going to go to jail for a very long time. You and Robles were pretty stupid dumping the body where you dumped the others."

"Others?"

"Yes, we also have the body of Manuel Muñoz." Helen pulled out a third photo. In this one, the coroner had placed the recently decapitated head onto the shoulders of the cadaver. "Do you recognize this hombre?"

Diaz looked at her and then at the photo. "Look, Señorita, we don' kill nobody. Ramon and me, we're *los transportadores*."

Helen looked at Baez.

"They are transporters…contractors who cart stuff away."

Helen turned back to Diaz. "So, you are admitting you and Ramon Robles received money to dispose of the three bodies?"

"Si, Señorita. But we don' kill nobody."

"Who cut the heads off the two bodies—Perez and Muñoz?"

"I was following instructions, Señorita. That is the way it was to be done."

"So, you chopped off the heads. Who gave you those instructions?"

Diaz dropped his eyes and began to sob. "I cannot tell you or they will kill me."

"You're going to go to prison, where you will be protected."

"They will kill me wherever I am, especially in *la prisión*."

"Who? Who are you afraid of?"

"El Serpiente."

Helen looked at Baez again.

Baez looked behind himself and then whispered, "The Serpent."

Helen cocked her head.

Baez realized she did not understand. "The snake, the viper, the serpent…it is the nickname of a man with great power in our community."

Helen remembered Roxanne Windsor's Black Hat Society told her to look for the snake. "What is his real name?"

Baez motioned she should ask Diaz.

Helen turned back to Diaz. "What is his real name, this El Serpiente?"

"I don't know. That's all anybody call him. If I knew his real name, I could never tell you, but Ramon may know."

"Why could you never tell me? Are you afraid of this man?"

"Yes, I am afraid. I took a blood oath of secrecy and if I break the oath, my head will roll like the heads of those other hombres." Diaz studied Baez for a moment and then turned back to Helen. "You should be afraid of El Serpiente, too, Señorita. If he knows you are on to him, your head will fall from your shoulders like all the others. Do you wear a steel collar?"

Helen went to the door and knocked on it. The guard opened it. "I'm done with this one," she said. "I want to speak with Robles."

****

Helen and her interpreter, Manuel Baez, waited until Ramon Robles had been moved into Interrogation Room Two before entering. Robles was a smaller man than Santiago Diaz. He was no more than five feet five inches tall and weighed under one hundred fifty pounds. His hair and eyes were the same shade of dark brown. He was clean shaven and the only mark on his face was a small blue tattoo of a scorpion at the base of his left sideburn. Like Diaz had been, Robles was shackled to the steel table and the floor. He looked angry.

"Good morning, Mr. Robles," Helen said as she entered the room. "My name is Officer Martin. The gentleman with me is Manuel Baez. He will act as interpreter if you don't understand the questions I ask. Do you understand what I've said?"

"Si, mamacita."

Helen gave him a sour look. "Cut the wisecracks."

Robles lay against the back of his chair.

Helen sat down. Baez sat beside her.

"Do you know why you have been arrested?"

"They say I killed some hombres and left them to rot in the woods. But I didn't kill nobody."

Helen had heard this before from Diaz. "But you will admit to dumping the bodies in the woods?"

"Who say I do this thing?"

"We already have a written affidavit from Santiago Diaz swearing you and he transported three bodies to a hillside near Mariaville, where you tossed them from your truck onto a hillside."

"Pasquale say that?"

"Yes."

"It was an El Camino."

Helen stopped short of berating him for his sarcasm. She pulled out the pictures of the three dead men and placed them in order of discovery in front of Robles.

"Can you give me the names of any of these men?"

Robles tilted his head and shrugged his shoulders.

"Could Pasquale?"

"Look closely, Mr. Robles. We need confirmation of their identities."

"I don't know any of these hombres. I just drove them up the mountainside and rolled them into a ravine, like I was supposed to do."

Helen pointed to two photos. "This one is Jorge Perez and the other one is Manuel Muñoz. And you don't know them?"

Robles shrugged his shoulders.

"Who ordered you to dispose of the bodies?"

"It is my job to discard unwanted merchandise. That's all…just my job."

"Who hired you to dispose of the bodies?"

"I don't know."

"Sure you do. It was El Serpiente, wasn't it?"

Robles' face froze and his eyes widened. "Did Pasquale tell you that?"

"Mr. Robles, you are going to go to prison for life if you don't tell me the name of the person who killed these men."

"Life in *la prisión* is short for men who can't keep secrets."

"Did El Serpiente kill these men himself, or did he order someone else to do it?"

"Listen, lady, you got someplace to keep me safe from El Serpiente? I doubt it."

"The city participates in a witness protection program. If the information you give me is valuable enough, maybe you could go away somewhere with a new name and occupation."

"And what about Pasquale? Is he already in your program?"

"There might be room enough for him. But you need to be forthcoming."

Robles shuffled his feet. The chains binding them to the floor shackles rattled.

"Who is El Serpiente, and did he kill these men himself?"

"Those three hombres all died in a question and answer session El Serpiente had with them. There was another, but you'll never find him."

"Why?"

"He's like that song...dust in the wind."

Helen looked at Manuel Baez. "What does he mean?"

Baez spoke a few words to Robles. Robles replied. It was lengthy.

Baez turned to Helen. "The fourth man he disposed of went through a woodchipper. He's all over the yard behind Robles' home. If the woodchipper hadn't clogged, all the bodies would have been discarded that way."

"How awful."

"But Robles maintains he didn't kill the men. He and Pasquale were tasked with disposing of the bodies."

Helen turned back to Robles. "Who is El Serpiente?"

"Only if you promise me on your soul you can get me into your protection program..."

Helen rose from the table and walked out of the room. Ten minutes later she returned.

"You'll get into the witness protection program if the information you give me leads to the arrest and conviction of their killer."

Robles looked closely at Baez, then turned back to

Helen. "Ask him to leave and I'll tell you what you need to know."

Helen nodded at Baez. Baez rose and walked out of the interrogation room.

When the door closed and he was alone with Helen, Robles gave her the name she was seeking. "El Serpiente is his name. He lives in Albany. He is a bad man, Señorita. A very bad man."

"His real name?"

"Señor Dario Estrada."

"And he killed those three men?"

"They died during interrogation, Señorita. He killed all four of them. You forgot the one who isn't in your pictures."

"Yeah. But you don't know their names?"

"No, Señorita." He raised his hands against the cuffs which bound them and held them as if praying. "But my life…it is in your hands."

Chapter Thirty

French called me at nine on Friday morning. I had just finished squeezing caulk into the bullet holes in the walls of my cabin and was sitting outside in a folding chair drinking a cup of coffee and watching loons playing in the water.

"Come in pronto, Jones," he said.

He seemed troubled. I hoped I had done nothing to upset him.

"I'll be there in half an hour."

"Make it quicker."

I decided to forego showering and shaving. I poured my fresh cup of coffee into the sink, grabbed my car keys, and headed to Cabrillo Construction. The guard at the gate waved me through without inspecting my Bronco. He must have known I was coming, and French must have told him to let me pass without the usual search.

I pushed the front door open and walked into the showroom.

"Good. You're here," Laverne said. "He's anxious to see you."

She hit a button and the door to the work area popped open. I headed into French's office without hesitation.

Caesar's face was flushed, and his eyes were teary. My usual chair was occupied by a young man I had seen before but didn't know. His face was contorted with anger.

I sat in another chair. "What's wrong, Caesar?"

"Did you tell anyone about your meeting with Rosalita Vieques?"

"Of course not."

"Not even that detective friend of yours?"

"No. Nobody." I thought for a moment. "I asked Helen to run a background check on Dario Estrada, but I didn't tell her where I obtained his name."

French slammed his hand on his desk.

"What's wrong?" I asked again.

"Rosalita was found dead in an alley in Albany this morning."

"Oh, God. And she was so afraid of the consequences of speaking with me."

"Her head was severed halfway from her body. Whoever killed her left her to bleed out."

"It had to be Los Cuernos…Estrada. He delights in severing heads."

The young man in the other chair punched his fist into the wall beside French's bookshelves. A shelf collapsed. Several books and glass trinkets from third world countries clattered to the floor. "I am sorry, El Escondido. Rosalita was the love of my life. On my mother's grave, I beg you to let me in on any plans to kill El Serpiente. That *bastardo* deserves to be peeled alive."

French placed the fingertips of both hands to his forehead and sobbed. "She was an innocent child. All she did was give us the name of the local leader of Los Cuernos, and she was executed."

As I had seen in the past, French loved his men and became emotional when they underwent difficulties or misfortune. I placed my hand on his desk. "There has to be a mole in your organization, Caesar—someone who reports back to Estrada. Whatever plan we devise to capture El Serpiente must be between the two of us and us alone."

"Yes, you're right. I trust your judgment on this matter." He looked at the young man. "Galtero, give me some time with Mr. Jones. I promise you will have your revenge."

Galtero stood and left the room, closing the door behind him.

"Was he Rosalita's—?"

French nodded. "Yes, they were lovers. They planned to marry in the spring."

"No wonder he's so upset. You'll have to introduce me sometime."

"Yes. I'm sorry I didn't attend to formalities. I am just so distraught about Rosalita's death. She was a beautiful young woman. Galtero will never find a woman so gracious and talented to replace her."

"So, let's capture El Serpiente and let Galtero avenge her death…"

"Yes. But El Serpiente will not fall into any trap easily."

"…and let's find your mole in the process."

French nodded thoughtfully.

****

Saturday evening we launched the plan. I drove French into Albany and circled the parking lot at Holy Redeemer Roman Catholic Church. Estrada's Escalade was parked near the door, and his driver was sitting behind the steering wheel smoking a cigarette. I stopped my Bronco behind the Escalade and backed into it, bumping his bumper with my trailer hitch. The driver got out angrily and approached my door.

"Wha' kinda stupid asshole are you?" he snarled at me.

I climbed out and glared angrily at him. "Your car is sticking out too far. It's too big for the parking space."

He looked at the round ding in his bumper. "You gonna have to pay for that, cabrón. Gonna be two thousand dollars at least."

French climbed out of my Bronco and examined the ding. It was two on one. "You can fix that ding with a small suction cup and some wax. It's no big deal. I'll even buy you the suction cup." He pulled his wallet out of his pants pocket and waved a twenty-dollar bill at the guy.

The driver became incensed and stepped into French's personal space, pressing his face as close as he could to intimidate him.

French smiled. "You been eating smoked onions, gordo?"

The driver pushed Caesar's chest with both hands, sending him into the side of a blue Volvo which was parked in the next space. Caesar pulled a pistol from his shoulder holster and pointed it at the driver, who raised his hands quickly and waved them in the air. "No, señor. I beg you. My employer wants his Cadillac to have no flaws. That's all I meant."

While French was dealing with the driver, I placed a magnetic GPS transmitter under the Cadillac's right wheel well and another behind its front bumper.

French waved his pistol up and down. "On your knees, maricón."

"Please señor…" French waved his pistol in an up

and down motion again.

The driver knelt before him.

"I have a message for your boss, El Serpiente. Tell him Rosalita's death will be avenged."

"Señor?" the driver begged.

"Do you understand the message?"

The driver nodded. "Si, señor. Rosalita…vengeance."

French handed me the pistol. I held it pointed at the driver's head. Then French removed a tire iron from the back of my Bronco and smashed the Escalade's rear window.

"Oh, no…" the driver moaned.

French tapped the driver's shoulder with the tire iron. "The angel of mercy smiles upon you, *maricón*. I will not kill you today because you must deliver the message to El Serpiente, comprende?"

Tears streamed from the driver's eyes. "Si, señor."

"Remain on your knees until we are gone from this church."

We climbed back into my Bronco and drove to Willow Falls.

At Caesar's suggestion, I parked my Bronco outside the Village Pub on Huron Street.

It was a sports bar with four televisions playing team games, mostly baseball and professional lacrosse. Two televisions were playing events broadcast from the Olympics in Japan. And two others featured local news and weather.

When the waitress asked our pleasure, Caesar ordered a double tequila. I opted for local draft. She brought our drinks and then we quietly discussed what we had done in the church parking lot.

Caesar sucked half of his tequila into his mouth, swished it around, and swallowed. "Best thing about the church is they don't usually have trouble from their patrons, so there's no video cameras taking pictures to identify us to the police."

"You scoped it out ahead of time?"

"Of course...but I'm not always so cautious."

The door to the bar opened and Galtero entered with two other men. They were all dressed in black denim pants and jackets.

"Ola, Galtero," I said.

"No names," Caesar said.

I felt like I had been scolded.

Galtero and the two men pulled up chairs and sat with us.

"Were there any complications?" Caesar asked.

Galtero shook his head. "It was easy."

The waitress brought Caesar and me another round of drinks and then took orders from the three men. All of them asked for beers. I was in good company.

Then a guy at the bar pointed at the television carrying the local news. "Hey, Barney, didn't you help frame out that place?"

I looked up. The screen showed an executive ranch house consumed in flames. Thick black smoke billowed into the midday air. Firemen from two stations had responded to the alarm. Then I recognized the neighborhood. "That's Estrada's home!"

Caesar nodded. "Yeah, it is. I wonder what happened?"

Galtero smiled. "Maybe he left a coffee pot plugged in or left a roast in the oven."

Caesar snickered. "Think I should call him to offer

him condolences or a place to stay? We trash guys gotta support each other."

The other men smiled.

Phase one of our plan was now complete.

****

Helen called me the next morning. "We've got the warrant, and we're going to go arrest Estrada for murder. Two squads. I can't let you come along because you're not with the department, but if you park down the street, you can watch the fun."

"I think you're a day or two too late."

"What do you mean?"

"Don't you watch the news? His house burned down yesterday. It was almost lunchtime."

"You're shitting me."

"No. Check it out yourself. You maybe ought to touch base with the local hotels to see where he's staying."

"Son of a bitch. We've got testimony linking him to three murders. Do you think he torched it himself on his way out of town?"

"No clue, Helen. I just thought I could save you a trip to Albany."

****

Dario Estrada looked like a man whose private piece of paradise had just been condemned as uninhabitable. His eyes were swollen and dark from lack of sleep. His hair was unkempt, and he had not shaved. He was dressed in tan Bermuda shorts and a gray sleeveless undershirt that exposed the thick crop of dark hair which covered his chest and shoulders. Standing with a small group of men in the dew-soaked weeds of a non-working farm somewhere among the Amish properties in rural

Montgomery County, his feet were protected from stickers by the thick soles of Hirachi sandals. With him were his two personal bodyguards, Toledo and Mateo; his accountant, Jaime Rothstein; and his attorney, Lance Freeborn.

"What did the cops want?" Estrada asked.

"They have issued a warrant for your arrest," Freeborn said.

"On what charge…arson?"

"No. They have accused you of the murder of three men—the three whose bodies were found in the woods near Mariaville."

"Nonsense. I didn't kill anybody." Estrada swatted a mosquito away from his sweaty forehead. "Can't they see I'm being framed? Somebody blew up my business establishment and then burned me and my family out of our home. Find that person and you'll find the murderer."

"I'm working on your defense as we speak, but sooner or later you're going to have to turn yourself in. Hiding out like this does not paint a picture of innocence."

"Somebody is trying to kill me, probably that bastardo from Scentless Waste Management. Maybe you should put some investigator onto finding evidence against him and you'll find what you need to exonerate me."

"Didn't Mr. French offer to help you after the explosion?"

"That wasn't an offer. He was taunting me the way a bully taunts a kid in a schoolyard."

"Well, I'll see what I can do. At least it's a direction to begin. Meanwhile, I'm going to be spending a lot of time avoiding the police. My only protection is client-attorney privilege. I'm sure they have a tail on me at all times. They even may have tapped my phone."

"Are you sure they can't get you to tell them where I am?"

"Positive. Back in the seventies, the courts upheld the principle of attorney-client confidentiality when the attorneys of mass murderer Robert Garrow found the bodies of a few of his victims but did not give their locations to the police because doing so would incriminate their client."

"I didn't kill anybody," Estrada repeated.

"I didn't say you did. I'm only trying to prove to you that I don't have to disclose your hiding place. It's up to the police to find you without my assistance."

"Good."

Estrada turned to his accountant. "And what about my home? Did you contact the insurance company? How soon can we hire a contractor and begin reconstruction?"

Rothstein cleared his throat. "Your insurance company is cooperating with the fire department's investigation into the cause of the blaze. Their early findings include the use of an accelerant to spread the fire to every room. That usually points to arson."

"But I didn't burn down my home. Why would I do that? Besides, I was in church."

"They're looking into your business dealings, especially your debts, and into your habits."

"Habits?"

"Yes. For example, are you a habitual gambler and are you in debt because of it? They were surprised to learn you paid for your home with cash."

"It was a legitimate transaction."

"Yes, but who carries a million dollars around in cash? They suspect you of illegal activities and if they can prove it, your home and money both will have gone up in flames."

"You told them I won that money in a legal church lottery in El Salvador, didn't you?"

"Yessir, but they are still going to investigate your claim. The government of El Salvador is not being very helpful. And, until the insurance company is satisfied you're not covering up some form of illegal activity, they won't release the money to rebuild your home."

Estrada pounded his right fist into the palm of his left hand. "Sons of bitches."

"Where is your wife?" Freeborn asked.

"She and Carmella are staying at the Hilton. It's got an indoor pool and free wi-fi, so Carmella can do her homework. Their bodyguards are always nearby in the hallway."

"Good. I'm sure the police are monitoring their movements. You should not try to see them until this mess blows over."

"Si. Do you think I was born yesterday?"

"No offense intended. I'm just trying to protect you from unwise activity."

"Si."

When Freeborn and Rothstein had driven away, Estrada spoke with his bodyguards. "What new information do you have for me?"

Toledo was the first to speak. "Orlando says the guy who drove into the warehouse and took pictures of us painting the Scentless trucks was driving a blue Bronco."

Matteo pointed his finger at his boss and then quickly brought it down. "No disrespect intended, El

Serpiente. When we shot up the cabin on Mariaville Lake, there was a blue Bronco parked outside. We thought we killed that guy. He must have the lives of a cat."

Estrada's eyes lit up. "As I suspected, El Escondido is behind all this misery."

"You want us to go back out there and kill that guy?" Toledo asked.

"Burn his cabin to the ground, Matteo and bring his head to me. Toledo, you stay beside me and remain ever vigilant."

Chapter Thirty-One

On Thursday evening, French drove out to Mariaville and picked me up. We had decided I should not be seen near Cabrillo Construction for a few days, and the presence of my Bronco would be a dead giveaway of my whereabouts. So, I left it parked at my cabin, and he drove me back into Willow Falls in a rented Nissan. He parked in an alley behind a row of empty buildings. "Here we are, amigo," he said before opening his door. "Come look at what I've prepared."

French had set me up in a vacant office building across the street from the main entrance to Cabrillo Construction. It had been home to a Radio Shack retail store until the post-millennium, when major competition from Apple and online electronics vendors had rendered its products and services essentially useless. But the building was perfect for my purposes. It was well-wired for basic electricity, and beyond that, nobody paid any attention to it anymore. It was just another empty storefront in a dying part of the city.

Caesar had leased the empty building from Bank of America, which had been stuck holding it when Radio Shack went bankrupt. Our local cable provider wired the place with "turbo" internet, and Best Buy's Geek Squad had outfitted it with six new laptops, each loaded with GPS tracking software.

Caesar called a staff meeting at noon on Friday,

insisting all his soldiers be present to hear his lecture about staying sober, clean, and watchful while Cabrillo Construction awaited some form of retaliation from Los Cuernos, the security subcontractors for Onondaga Waste Management. During his thirty-minute lecture, I placed magnetized GPS transmitters on the underbellies of the five vehicles driven by the men he suspected might be his organization's mole. The sixth was already on Estrada's Escalade. Then I went back into the Radio Shack building and watched the six monitors which were perched on two folding tables in front of my high-back computer chair. On the wall behind me was a refrigerator which had been well-stocked with sodas, beer, and several foot-long subs. To my right was a cot with pillow and blankets, and the Radio Shack's staff bathroom was fully functional, except it offered no shower.

At three in the afternoon my cell phone rang. It was Helen.

"Hey, sweets. What's up?" I asked.

"You never call me out of friendship anymore, Jonesy. We got to catch up. You want to come over for dinner?"

"I'd love to, but I'm on a special stake-out for a few days."

"Anything you can tell me about?"

"Wish I could, but I've signed a non-disclosure agreement."

"Why do you keep signing those things? Someday you're going to wish you hadn't."

I returned her question. "You got any news *you* can share?"

"Well, maybe you can help. Those two guys who dumped the cadaver for you implicated their boss. His name is Dario Estrada. You know we got an arrest warrant out him. Funny thing, though…after his house burned down, he went into hiding. Can't find him anywhere. We got tails on his lawyer and peeps watching his wife at the Hilton. But she's got bodyguards and we can't get near her. We've got to find that bastard Estrada before he skips out of state."

"I'm tied up at the moment, but as soon as I've wrapped this up, I'll do what I can to help you locate him, Helen. If anything pops up or I hear anything about his whereabouts, I'll let you know."

After Helen hung up, I watched the computer monitors for another hour. Then, finally, the little dots on the GPS map of the capital region began moving. That meant the workday was over, and Caesar's men were headed to home or other locations.

I could not have imagined how easy modern technology made it to identify someone's location. Some software lets a manager watch an entire fleet on a single monitor, but French did not want to monitor all his men twenty-four hours per day, and software of that caliber was especially expensive. He opted for the cheaper version, and he had to purchase one unit for each vehicle he was tracking. If he had accepted my advice, he would have opted for the expensive stuff and monitored all his men and his garbage trucks on a single computer. Whenever a truck was hijacked or the driver stopped someplace for a beer or a quickie, he would know where to find them. Go figure why he wouldn't do that.

As I watched, two of the drivers stopped in the barrio section of Schenectady. Two others went in opposite directions, one toward Albany's Afghani neighborhood and the other toward Saratoga Springs, where the Vietnamese population was increasing. The fifth driver drove west in an odd zigzag pattern. His erratic behavior instantly drew my attention. I called French. "Caesar, I think we've identified your mole."

"I'll be right over."

Five minutes later I watched Caesar's car leave the Cabrillo Construction compound. He turned left out of the gate and drove out of sight. Ten minutes later I heard a car door slam behind the Radio Shack building. It had to be Caesar.

He came through the back door. "Show me what we've got, Jones."

"It's your truck painter, Benito Varela. He's driving in circles, but slowly heading west toward the town of Fonda."

Caesar pulled up a chair and sat beside me so he could see the screen more easily. His breath told me he had recently eaten a mint. "How close is that to Estrada?"

"Estrada is in the country near the town of Glen, only a mile or two away. Varela's driving pattern says he's attempting to lose anybody who might be tailing him."

"Son of a bitch. And I trusted him, too."

"We don't know what he's up to. We have to wait until he's proven himself to be a traitor before we crucify him."

"Yes, but from his location we already know…"

"You're probably right."

We watched Varela's car move through the streets of Fonda, turning left, then right, and then left again, sometimes backtracking. He drove to the high school and then turned back toward town. Eventually he turned onto Route 30-A and beelined toward Glen, where he turned right onto Route 110. As we expected, two miles later his car stopped within one hundred feet of Estrada's Escalade. Phase two of our plan was now complete. We had our mole and, although we had known the location of Estrada's Escalade, we now were certain we knew where Estrada was hiding. We could take him out with a surface-to-air missile, but that was not our intention.

An hour later, our GPS software indicated Valera's car was moving back toward Willow Falls. French called him on his cell phone. "Benito, I got another truck for you to paint. Meet me at the painting shed at eight in the morning."

"Si, señor. See you then."

When Valera arrived at the warehouse in the morning, he was greeted by Galtero and three other men who frisked him for weapons and then escorted him inside to meet French and me. Valera looked alarmed. He should have been.

Caesar poked his middle finger into Valera's chest as he drove home his message. "You know, Benito, there's nothing worse than an hombre who pledges his loyalty and then goes behind your back to stab you. "

"Why are you telling me this, Señor French? You are frightening me."

"There is nothing worse than a mole, whose actions lead to the death of his compadres, a mole whose actions cost his organization thousands of dollars which could have benefitted the entire family."

"Why you accuse me of these things, Señor?"

"Do I kill you now in front of these men as a lesson in loyalty, or do I kill you later, after you've suffered for the death of Rosalita Vieques?"

Valera's eyes began to tear. His hands shook

uncontrollably. "Senor, please. I have done nothing disloyal. Please, do not accuse me of such things."

"And where were you yesterday after work?"

"Home with my family, Señor. I swear, I was home with my family."

"After you drove to the hiding place of El Serpiente and told him of our plans?"

"No, Senor. I know nothing of this. I have done no such thing. Haven't I always been loyal to you and Cabrillo?"

"When you left work yesterday, you drove to see El Serpiente. Mr. Jones and I watched you do that heinous thing."

"No, Senor. Juan and I drove to my home. He borrowed my…" Valera threw his hands up to his jaw. "Oh, no…not Juan."

Galtero stepped forward. "It's his brother, Mr. French. Juan Miguel is Valera's half brother."

French turned back to Valera. "Did Juan Miguel have your car after work?"

Valera's expression turned to horror. "Please, Senor, not Juan. We have the same *madre*."

French looked at Galtero. "Find him and bring him to me."

"Come, Pepe," Galtero said.

He and one of his compadres hurried away.

French pulled a pint of whiskey from his rear pants pocket. "Here, Benito. I apologize. I never should have doubted you."

Valera took the bottle, drank a healthy mouthful, and then coughed. "Our *madre*…she will never understand. But Juan's father is a drunkard and a liar. Juan suffered at his hand."

"Have some more, Benito."

Valera drank three more swallows.

"Go home, Benito. Be with your family this afternoon." French handed him a one-hundred-dollar bill. "Take your children to a movie and out to dinner afterwards. Let them see the love of a good father, as I have shown you the love of a father."

Valera took the money and sobbed. "Si, Señor French."

Half an hour later Galtero and Pepe returned with Juan Miguel. He was still in his blue and white striped pajamas. His face was bruised, and his lip was swollen as though he had been in a fight.

"Is it true, Juan Miguel?" French asked. He walked in a circle around the beaten man. "Is it true you do the bidding of El Serpiente?"

Juan Miguel held his head down in shame. "Si, Señor French."

"Why would you do such a thing?"

"On my mother's life, I did not plan to do this thing, El Escondido."

"Then why?"

"El Serpiente has my father and my other half-brother, Phillipe. If I do not help him, he beats them and has promised to kill them. He sharpened his machete in front of me. He held it at my father's throat."

"Why did you not come to me about this predicament?"

"Señor, I beg you…"

"You will now help me, or your half-brother, Benito, and your mother will suffer at my hand."

Juan Miguel fell to French's feet and nodded. "Si, Señor. Si."

"Are you well enough to drive?"

"Si, Señor. Si."

"Do you always drive Benito's car when you go to see El Serpiente?"

"No, Señor. I always borrow a different car, as El Serpiente instructed me to do. He is very wary of you. His men, they have plans to kill you."

French clutched Juan Miguel's hair and pulled it backwards so he could look into Juan's eyes. "And you did not come to me to tell me of this?"

Juan Miguel sobbed. "I learned this only last night, Señor."

"Today you will drive me to meet with El Serpiente. It is near the Town of Glen, yes?"

"Si, Señor."

"How many men protect him there?"

"Sometime four. Last night there was only one."

"Good." French turned to Galtero. "Have two men accompany Juan Miguel to the showers. Make sure they clean him up. He smells bad."

"Si, Señor."

"Then, choose three men to join you. Be certain they are armed with AK's and machetes. Select a good vehicle, something you can drive off-road. Be sure its tank is full. Meet me back here in two hours. We are going to capture El Serpiente, and you will have your revenge."

Galtero smiled, and then his smile became a sneer.

Chapter Thirty-Two

I stayed with French while he selected the vehicle which Juan Miguel would drive. It was an innocuous-looking green Chevy Equinox with blackened windows.

"This car has been modified with bulletproof glass and one-inch steel plates in its doors," French said. "The floorboard is IED-proof."

"Our boys could have used this in Iraq," I said.

"That's where I got the idea. We don't know what we're driving into. It could be a trap."

Galtero showed up promptly at eleven in the morning. He was driving a Toyota Land Cruiser. He and three companions stepped out.

"Good," French said to Galtero. "Have you briefed our men?"

"Si, Señor. We want to take El Serpiente alive. Anyone else can be wasted."

"Excellent."

Our two-vehicle caravan drove directly from Willow Falls to Glen, a small crossroads in the middle of nowhere. The Glen General Store sat at the intersection of two country roads. It was closed, probably a victim of the recent pandemic.

We turned right and drove for one mile. "Stop here, Juan Miguel," French said.

Juan turned on his blinker and pulled onto the weedy shoulder of the road. The Land Cruiser pulled in behind us.

French got out of the Equinox and walked back to give instructions to Galtero. "Remain at this position until you receive further instructions from me or Mr. Jones by cell phone."

Galtero nodded, not happy to be held back from the assault on El Serpiente. "Si."

French then joined me in the back seat of the Equinox. He waved a pistol at Juan Miguel. "Now take us to El Serpiente."

Juan Miguel drove slowly along the two-lane road until he turned onto a dusty driveway which led to a small brick ranch house, one hundred yards from the hard surface road. No vehicles were in sight.

"The place looks deserted," I said. "Do you think he knows we're coming?"

"We'll find out soon enough. We could be driving into Hell."

Juan Miguel stopped our car. Dust from the driveway passed by us in the breeze. Then a large man appeared from the side of the house. He was carrying a sawed-off shotgun.

Juan Miguel turned his head to speak to us. "That is Toledo, El Serpiente's bodyguard."

"Roll your window down so he can see you," French ordered.

Juan Miguel did as directed. "Ola, Señor Toledo. I came with new information for El Serpiente."

Toledo must have suspected something wasn't right. He twisted his head to look behind Juan Miguel. French pushed his revolver out the driver's window and fired twice, point blank range. I winced at the deafening noise. Toledo dropped his shotgun and stumbled backwards, his eyes wide open in surprise.

French and I quickly jumped out of the car. He went to the front door, and I ran to the side of the house. I heard the slamming sound of a screen door. I raised my semiautomatic and peered into the back yard. Nobody was there. Then I saw the top of a head bobbing and weaving through a field of thick brush.

"This way Caesar! He's escaping through the field in back."

French joined me in a few seconds.

"Which way did he go?"

"That way, toward the tree line."

"Many places to hide."

French pulled out his cell phone and punched in a number. "Galtero, see the tree line to your left? Yes, the one that is two hundred yards away. He's running there. Yes, he's alone. We'll follow his trail. You and the others fan out and try to cut him off."

French motioned with his hands. "You veer left, Jones. I'll veer right. Head for the tree line. We'll flush him out like a wild boar."

French and I began our pursuit of Estrada. The weeds were chest high and filled with prickly raspberry vines. The field was also dotted with six-foot tall pine trees. Estrada could be lying down anywhere, waiting for one of us to step into range so he could pick us off with a single, well-placed shot.

Without warning, several shots rang out fifty yards to my left. I kept moving toward the tree line in case Estrada doubled back. Twigs snapped to my right. I spun to fire. It was French.

"Caesar, I almost shot you."

"You've been trained like a cop, Gringo. You don't

shoot until you've identified the target. Some day you might be too slow."

"Any word from Galtero?"

"No. Let's fan out and move in the direction of the shots."

Two more shots rang out. Then a third. I heard a round pass by me as it struck through the thick weeds. I squatted down in case Estrada was firing at me. French knelt beside me.

Things became quiet.

"What do you think, Gringo?"

"I'll stand and see if I draw fire."

I stood. I saw motion in the weeds fifty yards in front of me. It was Estrada, holding his hands on the top of his head. Galtero and his three men pushed him forward.

"They've captured him, Caesar. Galtero has Estrada."

French stood. "Ola, Estrada," he shouted. "Nice you could join us for a walk today."

We waited for Galtero and his men to push Estrada up to us through the weeds.

Galtero was smiling like a man who had bagged the biggest game of the hunt. "He ran out of ammo. I found him crawling on his belly like a snake."

Estrada was a mess. His face and arms were scratched and bleeding. His clothes had been torn from thorns. He was missing one shoe.

"On your knees," Galtero ordered.

Estrada knelt, his hands still on his head. "Go ahead, finish it."

"We want you alive," one of French's men replied.

"Especially me," Galtero said.

French shook his head as we both approached. "You

know, Estrada, I would have found some way to do business with you, but you killed two of my most trusted men and Galtero's fiancé, Rosalita. And I promised Galtero revenge."

French turned to Galtero. "He's all yours, amigo. Take your time. Revenge should be thoughtful."

French and I wound our way back through the thickets to the Equinox. Juan Miguel was slumped over the steering wheel.

"Mother of God," French said.

He pushed Juan Miguel's shoulder. Juan Miguel fell over onto the console.

I saw what had happened. "Look at his wrists, Caesar. He slit his own wrists."

French pulled the body from his car. "He knew what was coming. He was responsible for the deaths of many men and for Rosalita's gruesome murder. He would have been next to die at Galtero's hand. I would have watched, but he stole the pleasure from me."

We dragged the cadaver onto the lawn. French pulled a machete from beneath the driver's seat, chopped off Juan Miguel's head, and threw it into the weeds for the birds.

"Good thinking," I said. "It's better the police think Los Cuernos did this to him."

Then we climbed back into the Equinox and drove to Cabrillo Construction.

Chapter Thirty-Three

French gave me a loaner car to drive back to Mariaville. It was an orange Chevy, probably a retired power company vehicle which he picked up for a song. Its steering was loose and its shocks were gone, but it would get me home.

I was tired and dirty and looked forward to cleaning up, even if it meant only a quick swim in the lake because my shower was full of bullet holes. I stopped short. My home and French's Bronco had been burned to smoldering cinders. As is the fire department's practice, a fire truck was standing by in case the fire re-kindled.

I parked at the edge of my lawn and approached the lone fireman on duty. "What the frigg happened?"

"Some guy's camp burned down. He was gunned down by somebody and his body was burned. Haven't found his head yet."

"Sounds like the script of a B-rated movie."

"You think so?"

I nodded. "Who was the guy?"

"The guy who rented this place was a retired detective from Willow Falls."

"You don't say?"

"Yeah. Troopers are on their way. So's some cop from Willow Falls."

The State Troopers arrived first. Two cars full of them. I watched and listened.

"Welcome, gentlemen," the fireman said. "Chief says he'll be right over if you need him."

"Probably don't have the time," the leader of the State Police squad said. "We've got to interview a few witnesses and we've got to investigate a missing person's report, too."

I turned at the sound of squealing tires. It was Helen. She was in uniform. She got out of her car, ran to me, and threw her arms around my neck. Then she kissed me passionately.

"You son of a bitch," she said. "I thought you were dead. I've never been so happy to see you as I am right now."

"Who's this guy?" the lead trooper asked.

"I'm Helen Martin, Willow Falls Police Department. This is Bartholomew Jones, the guy we thought was your cadaver."

"Probably intended to be your cadaver," I added.

"Then who's the cadaver?"

Another trooper stepped forward. "Possibly the missing person?"

"Hmmm?" the lead trooper muttered. "Go check with the lady in Cabin Thirty-three."

"So, what happened here?" I asked the lead trooper.

"You a cop?"

"Used to be. I now do private investigations."

"Do they involve Los Cuernos?"

"Unfortunately, they have recently."

"Well, I think they tried to do you in. They did somebody in, but we aren't sure who. At any rate, a neighbor lady of yours heard gunfire and saw an orange quad-cab full of men torch your home. She copied down the plate number and called it in. We apprehended the vehicle before it got to Albany. Had a shootout with them in Guilderland. Two of your assailants are dead. Two others are in custody. Come to find out, they're all tattooed with Los Cuernos stuff."

Helen hugged and kissed me again. "Don't know what I'd do if you weren't around as little as you are."

"Sorry, Helen. Been chasing down bad guys."

"Any news about Estrada?"

"Last I heard, he was hiding out in an abandoned farm near Glen. Give me a couple of hours and I'll get you an address. Got to find the place on a computer map. It's outside of the City, so you may have to cooperate with the State Police to go arrest him."

"Come home with me and get cleaned up. Looks like you're going to need some clean clothes and a place to stay. That can be with me for a few days. Jerry Astor isn't going to be too happy with what's happened to his camp. Maybe I can protect you from him."

I knew the burning of Jerry Astor' camp would only expedite the beginning of his new camp's construction, but I didn't tell Helen. Instead, I took her up on her offer, followed her into town, and moved in with her for the evening.

I was on her laptop computer using Google Maps to try to find an address for the place where Helen might find Estrada. At six thirty, Helen got a call from the State Police team leader. "As it turns out, the cadaver the firemen found was the missing person. He was a fifty-year-old man who went out for a walk and was just in the wrong place at the wrong time. His widow's a mess, especially since his head is still missing."

"How about the two guys you arrested in the shootout?" Helen asked.

"They haven't said much. They keep waiting for some guy called 'El Serpiente' to bring them a lawyer and bail them out. Bail for arson and murder won't be cheap, especially with attempted murder of police officers added to those charges."

"I found the address," I said.

Helen hung up with the State Police and looked over my shoulder at the computer screen.

I gave her the address. She immediately called the Montgomery County Sheriff's office. The sheriff returned her call fifteen minutes later. "You got a murder suspect hiding out in my county?"

"Yes, sir. About two miles from Glen. I need your cooperation to apprehend him."

Helen gave him the particulars about Dario Estrada.

"We'll have a warrant and be ready at first light," the sheriff replied. "Bring as many men as you think you'll need. We'll have eight. Meet us at the Glen Country Store. Do you know where that is?"

"Yeah."

Helen then called the Willow Falls PD and arranged for two teams of four men to meet her at the station at five in the morning. "We're meeting up with the Montgomery County Sheriff before dawn."

When she hung up, she turned to me. "Want to tag along tomorrow? I'll give you some special civilian title."

I was certain Galtero would have finished slicing the turkey by then. "Sure. It sounds like an adventure."

We talked until ten, and then I suggested we get some sleep. Helen lived up to my expectations. "You sleeping with me or you turning away a generous portion of soul food?" she asked.

"No offense, but we have an early morning tomorrow. We both have to be sharp."

"Always the Boy Scout, aren't you, Jonesy?"

I slept in her guest room on a twin bed with an oversoft mattress. Its sheets smelled a little like Mama Gracie's perfume, so I wondered if they were clean.

Helen woke me at four. "Coffee's on, stud-muffin. Get your ass out of bed." She laid a clean set of clothes at the foot of the bed.

"Where'd those come from?"

"An old boyfriend. He was about your size. But don't worry. They're clean."

I dressed and met her downstairs. "My god, I'm exhausted."

"Yeah, you were probably right about not bumping uglies last night."

We both sucked down a cup of coffee and then Helen drove us to the station. I stayed in her Hyundai while she briefed the men about our target. Then we were off, Helen leading the way to the Glen Country Store.

We arrived at the Country Store before the Sheriff and his entourage of Montgomery County's finest. While we waited, Helen walked between the two cars of Willow Falls Police, making small talk with the officers. There was an air of excitement and nervous energy among the men. And why not? Most of them had never been shot at before with anything except inaccurate Saturday night specials. Los Cuernos would probably be carrying automatic weapons and spraying rounds everywhere.

When the Montgomery County Sheriff arrived, he and his team of two cars blew by us, turning right onto Route 110 and leaving us in the dust. I swear I saw the sheriff flip us off as he drove by.

"Sons of bitches," Helen cried. "They want the collar and the credit for all our work."

The Willow Falls Teams started their engines, and we were off to the races. But we were thirty seconds behind the Montgomery County teams. By the time we pulled into the dusty driveway and came to a stop in front of the small brick ranch house, the sheriff and his men were already out of their vehicles and entering the house, guns pointed forward and flashlights beaming.

Helen pointed to a heap on the grass in the front yard. "What's that, Jonesy?"

"Let's go find out."

We exited Helen's car, pulled our weapons, and slowly approached the mass.

"It's a goddam cadaver, Jonesy."

"I can smell it from here. It's been in the sun awhile."

Helen pulled her flashlight off her belt and shined it on the cadaver. "Eeeww, its head has been cut off."

I looked. Sure enough, the head was gone. But I already knew that. Maggots were feasting on the rotting flesh of its neck. "It looks like coyotes or bears have fed on the thighs."

Helen turned to her right, bent over, and barfed. I handed her a paper napkin I had found in the front pocket of her ex-boyfriend's trousers when I was putting them on. I hoped Don Juan hadn't used it to blow his nose.

The sheriff appeared from the front door of the house. "Hey, Miss Willow Falls, the dwelling is empty. Somebody's been living here, but they're long gone." He stopped for a moment and looked at the mound beside us. Then he descended from the three-step stoop. "What you got there?"

Helen was still barfing.

"Something for you to tag and haul back to Fultonville," I said.

"From the looks of it, I might remand it into your custody for examination by your medical examiner. Got any ID on it?"

"This is your county and I'm just a tag-a-long observer. Maybe you want to turn it over and search it."

The sheriff turned and yelled toward the house. "Hey, Toby, fetch me a body bag and bring us a couple sets of gloves."

The voice of an unseen deputy answered, "Aye, aye, Sheriff."

"The sheriff shivered. "Finding a dead body gives me the willies, unless I shot the varmint who was formerly residing in it."

"Yeah, I know what you mean."

Helen stood and threw the balled-up napkin over her shoulder. "Thanks, Jonesy. You ever seen the deceased before?"

"How can I tell without a face? From the looks of it, we'll need prints and his wallet to figure out who he was."

A trooper appeared from the back of the house. "Sir, there's evidence of people moving through the field out back. Maybe they're hiding from us out there."

The sheriff nodded. "Figures. Why don't you take the Willow Falls men with you and see what you can find."

"Yeah, that's a good idea," Helen said. "Put my men out into snake and raspberry heaven." She turned to her men, who were leaning against their cars. "We need to search the field out back."

The men began to walk around the house. We could hear them talking among themselves but couldn't understand why the commotion.

"Detective!" one shouted. "We got another dead one in the side yard."

The sheriff, Helen, and I joined the congregated men. I could see it was Toledo, the man French had hit in the chest with two rounds.

"Look at the trail of blood," Helen said. "Looks like he crawled here from over by the driveway."

In the glare of the rising sun Helen had spotted an almost invisible trail of blood and crumpled grass.

"Good eyes," the sheriff said.

"Yeah, we female types are good at spotting dead men and assholes."

The sheriff gave her a questioning look.

I knew she was slamming him for his chauvinistic arrogance.

"Leave this one for the County guys," Helen said to her men. "It's a second one in their jurisdiction." She pointed toward the field. "Go see if you can find anything else of interest while the sheriff and his guys clean up this area."

"Be careful," I warned. "You never know what's hiding behind a bush."

The men dispersed, spreading out into a line so they wouldn't miss anything lying in the weeds. I watched them slowly searching the field for a few minutes and then turned to the sheriff. "Mind if I look inside?"

"Suit yourself, but don't touch anything. Not even a light switch. We're going to search everything for clean sets of prints. We want to know everyone who was hiding out here."

The inside of the house was less than I would have expected, given its most recent occupant was a regional gang leader. I would have expected better furniture and a nicer bed, but the home's two bedrooms each had only two cots with military mummy sleeping bags. The kitchen was clean, except for the trashcan, which was full of take-out meal bags and empty coffee cups. The living room was furnished with a portable television on a card table, an old vinyl sofa, and two reclining chairs in mismatched material patterns. The front window was covered by a hastily hung bedsheet. Clearly, the set-up was temporary—just something to accommodate Estrada until the heat was off. And I was certain his high-paid attorneys were busy working on his freedom at that very moment.

Fifteen minutes later Helen's cell phone rang. "Woods is safe," one of her guys told her, "but you're gonna want to come out here."

"What did you find?"

"Side of beef hanging from a tree branch."

"Execution by hanging?"

"No, nothing so quick or clean. This guy has been skinned like a deer, maybe while he was alive. You might want to bring the sheriff and another body bag."

Helen turned to me. "Jonesy, that was Beaudoin. We got another cadaver."

"Really? It's like an Easter egg hunt. They're everywhere."

The sheriff was talking with a couple of his men in the kitchen. Helen knocked on the doorframe. "You might want to bring a couple of strong guys and another body bag."

"Your guys find something?"

"Yeah, another dead guy. This one has been peeled like a grape."

"No shit?"

"That's what they told me."

The sheriff turned to two men. "Parker, you and Horstman grab another body bag and come with me and these Willow Falls officers into the field."

Helen and I led the small party through the field and into the tree line. We knew where we'd find the corpse because our guys were talking noisily.

The scene was just the way Beaudoin had described. The men were standing in a weed-free circle of trampled dirt, probably caused by intense shade from three towering maple trees. Dangling from the lowest branch of one tree was a bloody mess of fat and muscle, suspended by a rope which was tightly fastened under two salamis which must have been arms because finger-like appendages were attached to each end. Two bologna-like limbs hung from the mass, feet attached and toenails missing. I recognized the mass was a human body. Above the rope was a head, still attached to the neck, but all its skin was missing. The whites of its eyeballs were haunting.

I had no use for Estrada, but his death must have been tortuous and grisly. I found myself hoping he died quickly, but I think Galtero did not let him off so easily.

"Any idea who this guy might be?" the sheriff asked.

"Could be any one of a bunch of gangbangers," Helen replied. "Gonna have to run a DNA analysis and hope this guy is in the database."

"Sheriff?"

It was Horstman, one of the sheriff's men.

"Yeah?"

"You ever see human skin hanging on a bush?"

"I hope I never do."

"Well, it's your lucky day, sir. Got maybe forty pounds of it, hair and fat still attached."

Helen and I followed Horstman and the sheriff into a small patch of bushes, where a bloody mass of flesh hung from the boughs of an evergreen. A few small pieces lay on the ground. One could have been a face in the recent past.

"Jesus," Helen said, "this guy was really hated."

I shook my head. "Whoever did this showed him no mercy, Helen."

The sheriff sent Horstman back to get a second body bag, this one for the skin. "Maybe it'll have some distinguishing marks like tattoos or moles which will help us to identify him."

I nodded.

"I think we're done here," Helen said. "Estrada doesn't appear to be around. Think he could have done this?"

I touched Helen's elbow. "It's always possible the mass on the tree *is* Estrada."

"If it is, my case is closed. All I got is maybe six dead guys and nobody to accuse of murder." She paused for a moment and turned to look me in the eyes. "Are you trying to tell me something, Jonesy?"

I shook my head. "I think we're in unchartered territory, Helen. I'm just considering all the possibilities."

"Any idea who's behind all this?" the sheriff asked.

"Most likely Los Cuernos," Helen replied. "They

seem to be into headhunting."

We walked back into the clearing. Two of Helen's men approached her. "We've got something interesting to show you, Lieutenant."

We followed them to the body. It was still hanging from the tree limb.

"We opened the body bag under the corpse so we could cut the rope and drop the remains right in." He pointed at the inside of the open body bag. "Look at the stuff that's dripping off the body."

Helen bent down. "Smells like bacon."

"Yes, ma'am. And maybe honey, too. They've been smeared on the body."

I inspected the mass of raw flesh, prodding it with my finger. "Yeah, I think you're right. Half of the body is covered with grease and the other with sticky stuff. It's like the killer wanted to attract bears to consume the evidence."

"Don't touch it, Jonesy," Helen said. "You're contaminating evidence."

I wiped my finger on my trousers.

"And now you've got that bloody crap all over your pants, who you riding home with? I don't want that stuff in my car."

On the ride back to Willow Falls, I thought a lot about Estrada. Back when I was a police detective, I would have needed to bring Estrada to justice in a slow-moving criminal justice system which offered many exits to escape punishment, if he had enough money or wielded enough power. If Helen and the department could not prove Estrada's hand in the deaths of those men, he would walk. And the department would not even consider prosecuting him for Rosalita's death because it happened in another jurisdiction. To my mind, death by peeling was gruesome, but Estrada deserved it for all the deaths he ordered and/or committed. I was glad to have had a hand in helping him to meet his karma.

Chapter Thirty-Four

We were sitting at Captain Mambo's. Helen was eating a plate of fried haddock with cole slaw. I was eating the only thing I had ever ordered in that establishment—a fried shrimp platter with French fries.

"Were you just guessing when you said the guy in the tree might have been Estrada?"

I took a sip from my glass of sweet tea. "Yeah. Isn't it strange how some investigations end? I really didn't think it was Estrada, and then 'Bingo!' he turns up as the cadaver."

"I think you know more than you're telling me, but I'll let it slide for now. You got any guesses about who did him in?"

"He was Los Cuernos, Helen. I've got that on good authority." I popped a shrimp into my mouth. "One of my contacts told me Estrada was behind the 'Garbage War.' "

Helen dipped a forkful of haddock into a paper container of tartar sauce and then stuck it into her mouth. "You mean like all those trashcans that got burned and the explosion at the Onondaga Trash headquarters?"

"That's exactly what I mean."

"Why would he do that?"

"I don't know. Maybe he was hired by the Banditos to drive both companies out of business so they could expand their enterprise into Upstate New York. Maybe

Estrada wanted to take over the trash business himself. I mean, everybody has trash, and nobody burns it in their backyards anymore."

"Well, he sure pissed somebody off."

"Yeah. Maybe his death was a warning from the Banditos or another gang. Or maybe it was somebody higher up in Los Cuernos who wanted to send a message to all his soldiers."

"Like, 'stay out of management's business'?"

"Yeah."

Helen wiped her lips with a paper napkin. "You think he offed all those guys we found up in Mariaville?"

"Yeah, I do. All except the homeless guy you got for me."

"The Chief is still upset about that. He still doesn't know how the cadaver found its way to Mariaville. The security cameras were blank. They didn't record anybody going into the morgue and stealing the body."

"How did you manage that?"

"I did a favor for somebody."

"Is that all you're going to tell me?"

"You don't tell me everything, either."

I nodded. "Yeah, I know."

****

I was planning to sleep over at Helen's for a few days—until I worked something else out. It was an awkward situation because I suspected she wanted me to be a permanent bed buddy, but I was holding out. My divorce had left me unsettled about getting into a serious relationship. And, of course, there was Roxanne Windsor, who was a great 'romp,' if I can borrow a word from her vocabulary.

I was driving Helen's car back to her home, when I

got a call from an attorney out of Amsterdam.

"Mr. Jones?"

"Yes."

"William Gurnsey, here. I'm settling the estate of Ms. Naomi Malbrook of Mariaville. I believe you knew her."

"Yes. I helped her with yard work from time to time. You know, like pulling weeds out of the water around her dock. Her death was indeed unfortunate."

"Yes, it was. Well, let me cut to the chase. Ms. Malbrook included you in her will. Mind you, you're not her primary beneficiary, but she did leave you a little something as a 'thank you' for your assistance."

"This is certainly unexpected."

"Well, a small group of us will be assembling at her home this weekend to read her will and to sprinkle her ashes into Mariaville Lake, as were her last wishes. We hope you'll join us."

"When will that be?"

"Saturday morning at ten o'clock. I've arranged for a pontoon boat to pick us up at her dock."

"I've never been to such a ceremony. How should I dress?"

"Oh, Naomi won't care how you dress. She was very informal, you know. You'll be on a boat, and the minister who will be leading us in a prayer of remembrance will be wearing cutoff blue jeans and a tee shirt." There was a pause. "He's my son."

"Oh, well thank you, Mr. Gurnsey. I'll certainly be there."

I turned the car around and drove to Walmart, where I hoped to get a few new items of clothing to wear. The fire at my cabin had consumed everything I owned.

****

On Saturday morning, I arrived at Naomi's lake house at nine forty-five. I was wearing a pair of new khaki trousers, a green wick-away golf shirt, and white no-name tennis shoes.

As I pulled to a stop, an orange cat ran from Naomi's back porch and hid under a lilac bush in her side yard. The cabin's lawn recently had been mowed.

The door to the cabin next door opened. Out came Marv and Anna Faulkner and their daughter Emma Rose.

"How are you, Uncle Bart?" Emma asked.

"I've missed seeing you folks, Emma."

I shook Marv's hand and gave Anna's cheek a polite peck.

A black Lincoln came into the driveway.

"That should be the attorney," Marv said.

"Is anyone else coming?" I asked.

"I don't think so. He told me we would be a very small party."

William Gurnsey awkwardly climbed out of the Lincoln's passenger door. He appeared to be in his sixties. His hair was white and combed backwards behind his ears. He was wearing tan Bermuda shorts and a multi-colored Hawaiian shirt.

The minister was maybe thirty. He drove the car and, yes, he was in cutoff blue jeans and a gray tee shirt with a depiction of the Last Supper printed across his chest.

"Hi, everybody," the minister said. "My name is Brother Ron."

He shook everyone's hand and then motioned toward the pontoon boat at the end of Naomi's dock. "Shall we get started?"

Emma Rose ran toward the end of the dock.

"Be careful, sweetheart," Anna called out.

Her warning was too late, as Emma Rose was already aboard the craft and sitting in the captain's chair before her mother finished shouting "sweetheart."

"Oh, let her be," Marv said. "Pontoon boats are as stable as a porch. She's fine."

"Are you sure?"

"If we owned a camp, a pontoon boat is the first thing I would buy."

We all climbed aboard the boat and found seats around its perimeter. Then William Gurnsey pushed us off from the dock.

"Emma, would you mind finding another place to sit?" Brother Ron asked. "I'm today's official captain."

Emma hopped up and ran to the bow of the boat, where she could lean against its aluminum railing and watch for ducks and fish.

Brother Ron sat down, engaged the boat's quiet electric motor, and negotiated the pontoon boat through the weeds and into deeper, clearer water. When we were approximately one hundred yards from shore, Brother Ron shut the motor and rose, holding a Bible in his left hand.

"Please rise," he said.

We all stood. I looked over the side. Only a few feet below the surface were thousands of weeds, standing at attention like green soldiers, their fingers reaching toward Heaven from the silty lake bottom.

"Lord God Almighty, we have come here today to commend the spirit of our friend Naomi Malbrook into Thy loving arms. We beseech Thee to accept her into Thy kingdom and to the Heavenly reward she so much deserves. Amen."

Gurnsey handed a ceramic jar to Marv and asked him to sprinkle some of Naomi's ashes into the lake.

Marv carefully took the jar from Gurnsey, twisted the lid free, and shook several ounces of sandy dust into the water.

Emma looked over the edge as the dust particles settled beneath the water's surface. "Goodbye, Mrs. Malbrook. We love you."

Marv kept the lid, but handed the jar to his wife, Anna. She, too, sprinkled several ounces of ash into the water.

Brother Ron raised his palms toward Heaven. "From dust we came and to dust we return."

Emma Rose pointed into the water. "Look! Look at the weeds!"

Marv's jaw fell open. "Well, I'll be. I've never seen anything like that."

"What is it, honey?" Anna asked.

"Look at the weeds. They're curling up and sinking toward the bottom."

I looked over the side. "Son of a—"

Gurnsey and his son peered over the side of the boat.

"Isn't that amazing," Gurnsey said.

"It's a miracle!" Brother Ron declared.

Anna handed me the jar of ashes. "Your turn. Naomi really liked you."

I held the jar tightly and sprinkled most of the remaining ash into the water. "Go get those weeds, Naomi."

I handed the jar to Emma Rose. "You sprinkle the last of it, Emma. You were her special friend."

Emma took the jar from me and looked inside. Then

Anna helped her turn the jar upside down so the remainder of Naomi's ashes could find their way into the water.

When Emma Rose was finished, Marv took the empty jar from her and reseated its ceramic lid.

We all stared over the side. The water around the boat was virtually weed-free.

"Have we drifted into deeper water, son?" Gurnsey asked.

"Nope, Pop. the wind has drifted us back toward Mrs. Malbrook's dock."

Marv and I both looked back toward her dock. Brother Ron was right. We now were closer to the dock than when we had begun sprinkling Naomi's ashes. And the weeds beneath us were curling up and dying as though somebody had poured a caustic acid onto them.

Brother Ron started the boat's motor and we cruised silently up to the dock. Marv stepped out and tied the boat's bow to the cleat on the dock.

Gurnsey held up his hands. "Now before we go our separate ways, folks, I need to advise you about the contents of Naomi's will."

We all sat down on the boat's plastic cushions.

Gurnsey pulled a folded piece of paper from his pants pocket. "To my friend Bartholomew Jones, I hereby leave my Subaru Outback and the U.S. military-issued forty-five automatic pistol my father carried in World War Two."

I was astounded Naomi would leave me an automobile, especially since my Bronco was now a pile of twisted steel.

"Oh, how nice," Anna said.

"To my attorney, William Gurnsey, I leave from my

savings accounts at First National Bank the amount necessary to cover his expenses in arranging for my cremation and the settling of my estate."

Marv and Anna nodded.

"As it should be," Marv said.

"To my friends Marvin and Anna Faulkner I leave the remaining money in my savings accounts."

Gurnsey looked over his glasses. "Mrs. and Mrs. Faulkner, I believe that amount will be close to three hundred thousand dollars, after my expenses."

The Faulkners gasped.

"I'm not finished yet," Gurnsey said. He held up the paper again. "And to my best friend ever, Miss Emma Rose Faulkner, I hereby leave my cat, Jake—"

Marv shook his head. Anna's face showed signs of instant distress.

"...and my lake home, with all its property and furnishings."

Marv and Anna gasped, rose, and hugged each other.

Emma Rose tilted her head. "What does that mean, Daddy?"

William Gurnsey bent down and looked Emma in the eyes. "Young lady, it means Mrs. Malbrook has given you her lake home. Your family now owns a camp on Mariaville Lake."

"Oh my..."

"And your friend Jake now belongs to you, Missy," Marv said. "Mrs. Malbrook has been very generous to our family."

"And what about those weeds, everybody?" I asked. "Is it possible Naomi is pulling weeds at this very moment, ensuring the entire lake will be free from

Milfoil?"

"If it's so, it's truly a miracle," Brother Ron exclaimed.

"We all saw it," I replied.

"Yes," Marv said. "The weeds are curling up and turning brown right before our very eyes."

Anna put her fingers to her lips. "Do you suppose? …Is it even possible?"

Brother Ron held one finger high in the air. "With God, all things are possible."

Chapter Thirty-Five

French called me at eight o'clock on Monday morning. "You coming in today, Jones?"

"Sure, if you need to see me."

"Make it ten o'clock. I need to talk with you about an opportunity that has presented itself."

Helen had already left for work, so I felt less conspicuous walking around inside her home in my birthday suit. I showered, dressed in the same clothes I had worn to help sprinkle Naomi's ashes, and then drove my new Subaru to Willow Falls.

The war zone gate was no longer at the entrance to Cabrillo Construction, and the guard towers were no longer manned.

I parked in front of the main office and smiled at Laverne when I walked in. "He's expecting me."

"I know," she replied. "Go on in. The door is unlocked."

I walked into the hallway and knocked twice on French's door.

"Is that you, Jones?"

I opened the door. "Are you expecting anyone else, Caesar?"

He smiled at me. "No. You're it for this morning."

"What you got for me?"

"Coffee? It's straight from Colombia. Arrived last night."

"Sure. Black."

He rose, poured me a cup of coffee from the drip unit on his bookshelf, and then returned to his seat.

I took a sip and smiled. "This really *is* good. No wonder you import it yourself."

"So, Pancho Villa has returned."

I set my coffee on the edge of French's desk. "Did he…?"

He motioned with his hand, waving it back and forth at his wrist. "No, nobody has been killed."

I breathed a sigh of relief. "I don't like knowing about these things that are secrets within your corporation."

"I know, and it's best that way."

French poured more coffee into his own cup and took a sip. "Pancho Villa returned to Willow Falls with a business opportunity. It could make me a very rich man."

I nodded, waiting for him to tell me more.

"Have you heard of Captagon?"

I shook my head.

"It's the jihadists' drug of choice. It comes from the Middle East, mostly from Syria, where Islamic soldiers use it before going into battle. It enhances their courage and makes them feel invincible."

"No doubt it's a banned substance in the USA."

"Yes, but even American soldiers take methamphetamines in order to stay awake longer during times of war."

"Not legally."

"Of course not, but they still do."

"So, what about this Cap…?" I couldn't remember the term.

Caesar smiled. "Captagon."

"Captagon," I repeated.

"So, I sent Pancho Villa to execute La Cabra but La Cabra sent Pancho Villa back to me with an offer. La Cabra has been contacted by a Syrian organization which will provide all the Captagon we can market. I have an opportunity to be the national distributor of Captagon in the USA."

"How's that going to work?"

"La Cabra will import the Captagon from Syria and then sell it to me. I will then sell it to American military forces. Everybody makes money. What do you think of that?"

I kept a poker face. I was surprised and a little alarmed. I should not have been surprised because I suspected French, like his predecessor, dealt in all sorts of illegal activities and products.

"I think Captagon will be easy to sell to American soldiers," French continued, "especially to Army Rangers, Navy Seals, and Marine Recon. They depend upon perfect performance, and Captagon will ensure that."

"I think our troops don't need this new drug. They're strong and invincible without it."

"Oh, you are so naïve, my friend. Your soldiers drink beer and whiskey like it's water, and there's no doubt they use performance enhancing drugs and steroids. How else do they grow all those bulging muscles? Captagon will simply be another tool in their arsenal, and they will eat it like candy."

"So, what do you want from me?"

"Nothing…yet. I only wanted to see your reaction. I have already set up a meeting with two Army Rangers from Fort Drum. They will be my beta test. If they sell what I give them and their comrades want more, sales will increase very quickly."

"You already run two successful legitimate businesses, Caesar. Think carefully about this opportunity. Are you really ready to go there?"

He smiled at me, but he said nothing.

His phone rang.

"Hello?…Yes…"

He waved me away and covered the phone's mouthpiece. "This is personal."

I left French to his latest joy, thoughts of the millions he would rake in as the national distributor of imported Captagon. This venture was going to open new doors for both of us, doors which I knew should not be opened. If there is a Hell, then the Captagon doorway would probably lead there.

On my way back to Helen's, I drove past Willow Falls Ford. Sitting under the awning was a brand new Ford Explorer, white, with black wheels. It was hot looking. I pulled into the lot to test drive it. I learned it was the current year's model, but it had been returned because the buyer's wife didn't like the wheels.

"She thought it looked like a gangbanger's car," the salesman told me. He was a short guy wearing a black suit with dandruff collecting on his shoulders.

"Why didn't she just have the wheels changed?"

"Beats me. We offered to do that, but she was incensed her husband would buy a car without consulting her."

"How many miles?"

"Twelve hundred."

I test drove it, got a nice trade-in on my hand-me-down Subaru, and drove out the door with my new car an hour later. I financed it through Ford, and I thought it was a sweet deal.

Once again on my way back to Helen's, I thought of Roxanne Windsor. Conscious of not wanting to break the law, I pulled over at a Stewarts Shoppe and punched her number into my cell phone.

"Bart Jones," she exclaimed. "What a surprise. What would prompt you to call me?"

"I just bought a new car and thought maybe you wouldn't mind being seen in it with me."

"Is it a Tesla?"

"Well, no."

"Is it a Jaguar…a Maserati?"

"Come on, Roxanne. You know me better than that. It's a damn Ford Explorer, but it's a hot number."

"Oh, I can just see you in an Explorer. You with your gun out…chasing bad guys."

"Listen, Roxanne, I was wondering if you'd like to go out to dinner with me this evening?"

"No, I'm sorry, but it's out of the question. However, I'd love to have you for dinner at my place. Say seven o'clock?"

"Sure. I'll bring wine."

"Fine." She paused for a moment. "Oh, Barty, would you mind stopping by the store and picking up a bottle of baby oil. We might need it…"

I texted Helen:

—Don't look for me tonight. I've got a stake out.—

A word about the author…

Born in Massachusetts, Edward Baker traveled widely as a child because his U.S. Marine father was transferred on a regular basis to new assignments across the U.S.A. By the time Ed was twelve, he had crossed the United States three times. And as a licensed driver at the ripe old age of sixteen, he drove a stick shift Ford across the nation, following his dad, who was pulling a camping trailer behind the family's station wagon.

An English major at Elon College, Ed earned a master's degree at Appalachian State University and a doctorate in Educational Leadership at the Sage Colleges' Esteves School of Education. After thirty-five years in higher education and after retiring as Interim President of a public community college, he turned his attention to his first love, writing, while continuing to teach undergraduate and graduate courses on an adjunct basis at a private college in upstate New York.

During the cold months, Ed and his wife "hole up" in their winter quarters in Saratoga Springs, New York. However, during the warm months, they reside in their cabin on Galway Lake, New York. When he's not writing or engaged in a woodworking project, Ed can be found on the lake or playing with his grandchildren or his four-legged canine companion Sudsy.

For more about Ed or to read his blog, see Ed's website at: www.edwardsbaker.com

Thank you for purchasing
this publication of The Wild Rose Press, Inc.

For questions or more information
contact us at
info@thewildrosepress.com.

The Wild Rose Press, Inc.
www.thewildrosepress.com